Can the best of friends ever be more. . . ?

Pearl came to the door, picnic basket in hand and smiled. She was lovely in the yellow dress. Yellow like the sunshine; it was his favorite color.

"Are you ready?"

Pearl smiled. "Yes."

"Shall it be down by Johnson Creek?" he asked, assisting her up into the buggy.

"Yes, it's my favorite place."

"I feel I should be working." Paul took the reins.

"I feel the same way."

"You do need to think some things out," Paul said.

"Yes."

Pearl held her hands in her lap, wishing she could relax. Paul was her friend. A brother to her. Why was she finding it difficult to talk? Her feelings were strong and she wished she could take them back and just be his friend again. It was easier that way.

"Pearl, what is it you want to do?"

His question caught her off guard. "I don't know." How could she say how she felt? That she wanted to have a home, children?

"I think you do know. You're afraid of something. Why don't you talk about it?"

"How is Nancy Whitfield?" Pearl hadn't gone to church the past two Sundays. She'd stayed home taking care of Mama.

"Nancy is moving to Seattle."

"Are you taking a job there?"

He stopped, letting the reins fall. Suddenly it all came together. Nancy. She thought he cared for Nancy Whitfield. Didn't she know, couldn't she tell that he thought of her day in and day out?

BIRDIE L. ETCHISON lives in and well knows the beautiful Willamette Valley region that she writes about so colorfully in **Heartsong Presents'** "Willamette Valley Series."

Books by Birdie L. Etchison

HEARTSONG PRESENTS
HP123—The Heart Has Its Reasons
HP168—Love Shall Come Again

Love's
Tender Path

Birdie L. Etchison

Heartsong Presents

To Aunt Pearl, and especially Sarah, my great-grandmother, who brought her family to Oregon.

A note from the Author:
*I love to hear from my readers! You may write to me at
the following address:* **Birdie L. Etchison
Author Relations
P.O. Box 719
Uhrichsville, OH 44683**

ISBN 1-57748-009-0

LOVE'S TENDER PATH

Cover illustration by Peter Pagano.

PRINTED IN THE U.S.A.

one

Pearl Galloway stood on the station platform, body erect, wide-brimmed straw hat in hand. Her brown hair braided for the trip was in a coil at the nape of her neck, while wisps of hair framed the round, broad face.

She was going to fill the position of schoolteacher in a one-room schoolhouse in the farming community of Stayton, Oregon, nestled in the lush Willamette Valley. School did not commence until mid-October, when the harvesting was over.

Pearl had hoped for a school closer by, but a teacher was needed there, and it was time she became gainfully employed. Though she was not quite eighteen, she'd taken the mandatory two-week training, passed the test, and had been accepted.

Sarah Galloway's voice interrupted Pearl's thoughts. "Thee will be missed. If thee must know, it is all I can do to see thee leave like this. And so far away."

"Mama, fifty miles isn't far. I just wish it weren't so hot."

"Perhaps it will cool off by Monday."

The sound of the train chugging down the track, made Pearl's heart skip in anticipation. *I'd rather be married,* she wanted to say, rather than going off like this. But the words were locked tight inside her. She'd lamented once to Mama about not being a boy. "Since I look like a boy, I should have been one."

"I'll hear no more from thee," Sarah had said in her commanding voice. "One does not question God, Pearl Marie. If God had wanted to give me another son, then He would have."

The Galloway's hadn't been Quakers long, but Sarah used thees and thous regularly. Buxom and broadshouldered, she fanned her face while watching the train come down the track.

The train whistle sounded again and Pearl squeezed Sarah's hand. "Mama, how do I know I can teach? What if I fail?"

"There are no failures in the Galloway family," Sarah said. "Remember what I've always taught you: Quitters never win, and winners never quit. You are so good with children; you'll be a wonderful teacher."

"Oh, I hope so, Mama."

Ben lumbered up then. "Pearl, I'm sure going to miss you."

"And I, you." She smiled at her older brother. "Now you must give my nephew, Clifford, his piggyback rides. He looks forward to them, at least twice a day."

"I think I can handle that." Ben leaned over and hugged Pearl as the train rolled to a stop. He lifted the heavy trunk while Pearl showed her ticket to the conductor.

"Is one trunk all?" the conductor asked.

Pearl nodded. She didn't own much in the way of clothes. Four dresses, her old shoes and the good ones which she wore now. Buttoned up past her ankles, the shiny leather shoes had been Ben's farewell present.

"You can't teach without new shoes," he'd said.

Sudden tears filled her eyes. She'd never been away from Mama or her family. The one blessing was that she'd board with people she knew. John and Nina Colville, who used to attend the Friends Church in East Portland, now owned a farm near the Stayton School and had invited her to stay with them.

Pearl smoothed out the skirt of her dress. Made of navy blue lawn with sprigs of blue and lavender flowers, it was a gift from Kate Morrison. The custom used to be that Quaker young ladies only wore gray or dark colors, but times were changing and Pearl liked the brighter materials. It was fitting she would wear this dress as she traveled on the train to her first job.

Pearl hesitated on the step, ran back down and hugged Mama hard. Sarah had never looked so forlorn, as she did now with the sun shining out of a cobalt blue sky, encompassing her in a wave of heat.

"God go with thee, little one."

Pearl giggled, straightening the flower on her mother's hat. Little one. A misnomer if ever there was one. She'd always been tall and gangly for her years, and people often thought she was older than she was.

"All aboard!" called the conductor. Pearl clambered back up the steps and turned around once more to wave at her mother. Sarah was coughing into a handkerchief and Pearl felt a wave of uneasiness. The cough was lasting too long. Why hadn't it gone away by now?

Ben waved from a thin patch of shade by the station, where the team of horses stood, waiting. Soon they'd be back home, in time for the noon meal.

Pearl looked down the road as far as possible, hoping to see a certain someone come riding up. Why hadn't Paul come to say good-bye, to wish her well? Yet she was certain he had eyes for another—a small girl with laughing blue eyes and blonde curls cascading down her back. Why would he look at plain, tall Pearl?

If she'd been pretty like Nancy Whitfield, Paul Drake might have brought her to the train station—might have said he would wait for her return—might have asked if he could court her. But he had not, and now she must carry the memory of Nancy leaning on Paul's arm in church. Nancy at one end of the aisle, while she, Pearl, sat at the opposite end, wishing with all her might she could trade places.

She found a seat by the window and waved until her mother faded into the passing scenery. Pearl withdrew her hat, placing it on the rack overhead, then removed her best go-to-meeting gloves and put them in her lap. Now she could sit back and try to ignore the stifling heat that permeated the car.

The feelings for Paul were unexpected. They'd been the best of friends since his arrival in Oregon that night a year ago. Coming on the train from California, he'd found the Galloway home and been met by his sister, Emily, who cried with joy. Soon he was just part of the family.

When had Pearl's feelings changed? When had she dared to hope he might look at her in the special way Ben had for Emily, and their friends Luke and Kate had for each other? She tried to stifle the thoughts, but Paul's face came to mind often. The year that ensued had been one Pearl would carry always in her mind and heart. Pastor Luke and Kate's marriage—Emily and Ben's baby Clifford arriving with strong body and lungs. Nobody spoke of Isobelle, the baby born a year earlier, living only a few hours. How Emily had braved it, Pearl did not know. If it had been her baby— There she went again—dreaming the impossible.

She and Paul used to talk about a lot—evenings after work when he shared what he wanted out of life. Other times when he expressed his disbelief in a higher being. When she asked why he felt this way, he smiled in that shy, boyish way and said he had never seen anything happen to make him believe. This lack of belief bothered Pearl, but she kept it inside. Nobody knew, because he attended the Friends meeting each Sunday, because not to do so would have caused ire in Ben, his brother-in-law, and consternation, to Emily.

Yes, Pearl realized she had nothing to despair about. If God had intended for Paul to be her husband, he would have allowed her to find a teaching job closer. This going away was a test. Pearl would prove she was capable of being on her own, and in time she would put feelings for Paul aside. Besides, she had so much to be thankful for. If Emily could live through the death of her first baby and still love God—if Kate could have her heart broken twice by Jesse and find more love in her heart for Pastor Luke, Pearl had had nothing to face by comparison.

Forget about Paul. . . , forget about Paul. . . , forget about Paul. . . . , the wheels seemed to say as they clacked over the miles.

"'Count Thy Blessings,'" she hummed under her breath. "'Count thy many blessings see what God hath done.'"

"I like that hymn," a voice said suddenly from across the aisle.

Pearl turned and stared at an older woman with kind, gray eyes. "Pardon me, but was I humming aloud?"

The woman nodded. "Yes, you were. 'Count Your Blessings' is what we all must do. Seems we tend to forget how good God is and how he blesses us in so many wonderful ways."

Pearl's face flushed. "Yes, I find it to be so."

"You've certainly made this hot, windless morning much better, believe me."

Pearl leaned back and smiled. Yes, she was a child of God in every way. How dare she sit here feeling sorry for herself? She had a family who loved her. She also had a position to fill—children who needed to learn. She hoped they would be eager as she had been when she first arrived in Portland.

"And where might you be going?" the lady asked.

"To Stayton—to teach school."

"You'll be one fine teacher," the lady said. "Anyone can tell by just looking at you."

Pearl beamed. "Thank you for those kind words."

Her traveling companion was going further, to Eugene, but the two chatted about Oregon, the land, and the way the area was growing, and soon the train pulled into the Stayton station and Pearl leaned over and hugged her new friend. "May God go with thee on the rest of thy journey."

"And also with you, child."

Soon Pearl's trunk was taken off and the train pulled out of the station, leaving her on the deserted platform. A feeling of fear engulfed her as she stood, looking around.

Where was the man from the school board? He had promised to meet her train and would drive her to Stayton. Pearl fanned her face with her hat, and tried to ignore the way her new dress stuck to her back.

A sound of thundering horses hit the hot, still air and Pearl turned to see a man dressed in a suit and top hat alight from the carriage. He tipped his hat. "Miss Pearl Galloway? I'm Judson Rome, head of the Marion County School Board." He stood over Pearl, a fixed smile on his face. "Welcome to Stayton!"

Pearl held out a gloved hand. "I'm happy to be here, sir."

He shook her hand. "Sir won't be necessary. It's quite acceptable to call me 'Judson.'"

"Yes, sir, Judson," Pearl murmured.

He was tall with a determined stance, but it was the dark brown eyes with their sternness that made Pearl realize this man might be difficult to please. A sense of foreboding hit the pit of her stomach. He seemed to be sizing her up as he lifted the trunk into the back of the buggy. She couldn't tell if he approved or not; his mouth remained tight-lipped.

"We have a wonderful little school with sixteen pupils expected, as I told you in the letter—including three of mine."

Pearl twisted the handle of her valise. "I'm eager to

get started, sir. . .Judson. I understand the ride will be long."

"Yes, and unfortunately, a dry, hot one. I have brought a jug of water along."

Pearl breathed in deeply of the fresh countryside air. Newly harvested bales of hay filled pastures and an occasional barn and farmhouse was visible from the road. She'd forgotten how much she missed farmlands after living in the city the past three years.

"It's beautiful here," she said, holding on to her hat as the horses trotted over the rough dirt road.

"I'm glad you like it."

"Can you tell me about some of the students?"

He smiled, revealing a row of even, white teeth. "My children have no mother, so they may cling to you at first, but you are not to allow it."

"No mother?"

He stared straight ahead, giving the reins a severe crack. "My wife died a year ago. It was the flu. Several died in our little community."

"I'm so sorry—," Pearl reached out, but drew her hand back. "It must have been painful for you."

He nodded, but did not look her way for a long moment. "It was. I'm looking for a mother for my children. They *do* need a mother, and I a wife."

Pearl trembled unexpectedly. As if reading her thoughts, Judson changed the subject.

"You will teach arithmetic, English, reading and writing."

"I am prepared, Mr. Rome. . . Judson."

"We want only truths taught. Facts the students can

use in their lives."

Pearl nodded again. "I understand."

"Did I hear right that you are acquainted with the Colvilles—where you'll be boarding?"

"Yes, sir. They are Friends, as I am, and used to attend the Friends Church in East Portland. Fine people."

"I have heard they are, but I don't go along with the teachings of the Quakers."

Pearl swallowed hard. She knew people didn't understand the persuasion of the Friends, and she didn't care to discuss the reasons why. It was often best to say nothing.

"I am a Baptist," he said as if that answered the question sufficiently.

"Well, we all worship one God," Pearl said then, hoping the trip was soon to be over, feeling suddenly uncomfortable without quite knowing why.

"I'll pick you up each morning and deliver you to the school, Miss Galloway."

"Oh." She didn't know what to say to that.

"The Colvilles have one small wagon and that isn't suitable for a teacher to be transported. As you can see, my carriage is large. My sons will drive their own buggy to school each day, but I shall have Mary Alice ride with us. If not, people might talk."

"That is very kind of you, sir. Judson." *But I don't want to be indebted,* thought Pearl. How can I possibly let this man pick me up and take me home each day? She glanced at his profile, the chin set in a formal manner and shivered again. No, she couldn't allow this to happen.

"Mr. Rome, that is, Judson, I am used to a hay wagon; it's all we had on the Iowa farm I grew up on. I won't mind taking that to school."

His jaw tightened even more. "I want our school-teacher to have only the best. Believe me, it's all I can do to deliver you to this crude place these people call home. I wanted you to live in my house, but people would talk, without there being a chaperone, and as luck would have it, my housekeeper quit last week."

Pearl straightened imaginary wrinkles in her dress and wished the ride was nearly over. "I will be fine at the Colville's—no matter how crude the dwelling, and I'd be only too happy to take their wagon to school."

"Are you always so insistent, so determined in getting your own way?" His tone was almost surly.

Pearl raised her chin. "Sir, more than anything I want to be a good teacher."

"Yes, ahem. I suppose you know we have rules which you are to adhere to in the strictest of fashion."

"I'm sure there are rules, and I can assure you I will fulfill them to the best of my ability."

He handed her a slip of paper. "These were made in the year 1875, but they apply today as well."

Pearl unfolded the sheet of paper:

Rules for Teachers
Drawn up by the school board for the good of all, including teachers and pupils. All teachers being hired by this board will read and sign accordingly.

1. Teachers each day will fill lamps, trim the wicks and clean chimneys, if applicable.

2. Each morning the teacher will bring a bucket of water and a scuttle of coal or load of wood for the day's session.

3. Women teachers who marry or engage in unseemly conduct will be dismissed.

4. Men teachers may take one evening each week for courting purposes, or two evenings a week if they attend church regularly.

5. After ten hours in school, teachers may spend the remaining time reading the Bible or any other good books.

6. Every teacher should lay aside from each pay a goodly sum of his earnings for his benefit during his declining years so that he will not become a burden on society.

There was a line for her signature and the date.

Pearl read each rule twice, then took a deep breath. "There should be no problem as far as I can see," she finally said.

"Good. I'm glad we're in agreement on something, Miss Galloway."

I want to make a rule of my own, Pearl wanted to say. *Teachers will be responsible for their way to and from school.* But she said nothing, and they rode the rest of the way in silence.

Later, when Judson Rome pulled into the Colville's dirt yard, he jumped down and helped Pearl alight from the buggy, and carried her trunk to the front door.

"Thank you," Pearl murmured. She looked around and saw there were no flowers. No paint on the small house, but a curl of fire circled from the chimney and Pearl relaxed. Someone was home, at least.

"I will pick you up Monday morning at 7:00 A.M. sharp!"

And Pearl, realizing she would have to concede, at least in the beginning, retorted, "And I shall be ready at 6:55 sharp!"

The door flew open and soon Pearl was enveloped in Nina Colville's arms. "Oh, my dear girl, just look at thee. Thee is all growed up!"

Pearl stood back and stared at the friend she hadn't seen in over a year. There was a glow about her she hadn't remembered, and Pearl's heart pounded in thankfulness.

"So much has happened since we last saw each other." Nina poked a wisp of hair back into a loosely made bun. "We're finally starting our family. A spring baby, right along with the planting of the crops."

"Nina! What wonderful news! And perhaps I can help."

"Oh, Pearl, that would be wonderful. We'll be like sisters."

Pearl stared after the retreating buggy. Judson Rome hadn't even tipped his hat to Nina, nor had he said good day to Pearl. He was a most disconcerting, rude man.

"Did thee have a pleasant train ride?"

Pearl nodded. "But not as nice as the ride out through the hay fields. I do love the country."

"Thee will like teaching here then. John is still working, but should be in for dinner shortly. He can bring thy trunk in then."

Pearl was led to a makeshift bedroom in one corner of the square little house, with a curtain partition. She'd taken her faded brown muslin dress out of the trunk so she could change. Since there was no closet, the trunk would go under the bed.

She sat on the bed, a twinge of homesickness sweeping over her. Already she missed Emily, Ben's booming voice, Mama's smile and Clifford's chortle. And Paul. She didn't want to think about him, but there it was. In her mind. In her heart. And though he denied God's existence, there was room for questioning, room for growth.

But she must stop thinking about home and go visit with Nina. There were lots of things to talk about.

two

That first night in her new home, Pearl opened her Bible with trembling fingers. Whenever things were going wrong, she always found solace in God's Word, especially the Psalms.

The day swam before her eyes as she recalled the long train trip, what seemed like an even longer buggy ride with Mr. Judson Rome. She felt disappointment, not quite knowing why. His refusal to even speak to Nina Colville because she was one of those Quakers, made her realize he was worldly and lacked common courtesy. Courtesy was of utmost importance to Pearl.

Pearl began reading Psalm 30:5: "Weeping may endure for the night but Joy cometh in the morning."

After reading a few more verses, Pearl prayed for strength, wisdom and knowledge for the morrow. To be a good teacher mattered more than anything. She could not fail the children. She was here to teach and teach she would. The rudeness of one man, even if he was head of the school board, wouldn't change how she felt.

Paul's face came to mind as she slipped under the light cover. The heavy quilt would be needed later, but not now with the house still holding the afternoon heat. If things had been different, Paul might have considered her as more than a friend or sister, but it wasn't meant to be. By all indications, she was to be a teacher.

That was where her talents lay and where she was needed and Pearl needed to be needed. Tomorrow she would prove her mettle.

Morning came, and Pearl was more than ready. A low layer of clouds made everything look dismal. She shivered as she slipped into the sunny yellow dotted Swiss, the first dress Kate had made for her. If anything could cheer her up, this would. It fit nicely and was her second-best dress. Paul had commented once that she looked downright pretty in it. It was the only compliment he'd ever given her and she'd kept it close to her heart, treasuring the words from the man she cared about so deeply.

She dreaded the thought of riding with Mr. Rome, and realized this bothered her far more than the gray day. How far was the school? What would they talk about? He had said very little about his own children, though Pearl had tried coaxing some answers out of him. She wanted to know as much as she could about her charges. He had mentioned that his daughter's name was Mary Alice and that she looked exactly like her mother.

The teakettle whistled on back of the wood stove, and made the morning chill disappear as Pearl entered the middle room which served as a kitchen/dining area and front room.

"Good mornin', Nina," she called.

Nina turned and smiled. "Since this is thy first day, I thought we'd celebrate by having biscuits to go with our oatmeal."

Pearl washed up, nodding. "I'm just a mite scared."

"I know I'd be," said Nina, bringing the pan of

biscuits to the table. "Let's pray before thee leaves."

Pearl had thought of it already, knowing it would soothe her being.

After requesting God's help to watch out over Pearl and to bless each child that came, Pearl finished her oatmeal just as a noise sounded out front.

"Why he's early, if that's Mr. Rome," Pearl said. I wanted to help with these dishes."

"Don't thee worry one minute about them dishes. I don't mind. Thee just go along now and remember: hold thy head high and keep a smile on thy face."

The knock sounded as Pearl put a wrap around her shoulders. Fall mornings were cool and crisp and she knew it would be windy as Judson Rome drove his team hard.

"If'n you're ready, let's go," came the gruff voice when Nina opened the door.

"Won't you come in, Mr. Rome?" Nina offered.

"No need for that since I see Miss Galloway is ready."

Pearl took a deep breath, partaking of the beauty of early morning. She would smile and not let Mr. Judson Rome ruin this morning. It was then she noticed the absence of his child.

"And where is your daughter?" Pearl had so hoped to meet at least one child before the school day began.

"She wasn't ready. She's coming with the boys."

"Oh." So much for being chaperoned, Pearl thought.

Judson talked as the horses made their way along the well-worn path. Pearl listened, but her heart was on what she would do on her first day of teaching. She did so want to be a good teacher. She also hoped the children would like her. She had a sudden tickle in her throat, but she didn't cough.

The horses turned and suddenly stopped in front of a one-room building. The rough-hewn logs were new and Pearl remembered hearing this would be the first year for the school. Before Mr. Judson Rome could come around to assist her, she'd hopped down, holding her skirt high with her right hand, her left holding onto her satchel. She marched into the room and gasped. It was perfectly wonderful. Desks had been hewn out of logs and the floor was made of wooden planks—she'd half expected to find a dirt floor. A blackboard covered one wall and a flag hung from a pole in the corner.

Judson barreled in behind her. "I am not used to seeing a woman get out of a buggy on her own."

Pearl didn't respond as she went about displaying her books—the spelling, the reader, the arithmetic. There was chalk, a thick tablet and pencils. She didn't know if the children would have their own supplies and had brought extra paper for this first important day.

"I see you approve of our new school."

Pearl clasped her hands. "It's more than I dreamed about."

Judson Rome nodded. "And if it weren't for me, you wouldn't be here."

Smiling, Pearl held out her hand. "Thank you for giving me my first job as teacher."

"I shall return to fetch you later."

"And your daughter will accompany us?"

He didn't answer, but turned and stomped out the

door. It was a temporary truce.

Pearl had considered the possibility of walking the three miles to the schoolhouse. She could do it in less than an hour and somehow knew it would be far more pleasant to do so than to rely on Mr. Judson Rome to fetch her each day. But her mind was diverted with the arrival of the first few children. She asked each name as they came shyly in.

Mr. Rome's children were the last to arrive. Pearl knew it had to be them, as they were the only ones who had a team of horses and a wagon to bring to school. This she'd learned from the girls who sat in front.

The team was driven hard, and Pearl noticed the small figure hunched over in the back. They had probably frightened their little sister deliberately. All the more she should ride with us each day, Pearl thought.

"Do come in," she called brightly. "School's about to begin, so find a desk and tell me your names."

The room had filled with warmth, thanks to the fire Pearl started in the small pot-bellied stove. That was one thing she had learned when she was young: building fires. A lot of things had depended on her, back on the Iowa farm.

The boys shuffled to the back of the room while Mary Alice chose a seat next to Cora Gentry. The twins removed their coats, then came back to hang them on the nails on the north wall, tracking large clumps of mud across the new floor. Pearl winced. She could hardly ask them to remove their shoes. Tomorrow she'd bring a broom for sweeping.

Pearl went around the room twice, putting names to

faces. Sixteen pupils was a goodly number. While the younger ones learned the alphabet, she'd listen to the older ones read and work on arithmetic.

After the Pledge of Allegiance was recited, Pearl read the 100th Psalm from her Bible. Just touching her well-worn Bible gave her a small amount of comfort.

> *Make a joyful noise unto the Lord all ye lands.*
> *Serve the Lord with gladness!*
> *Come unto his presence with singing!*

A whisper sounded from the back of the room, but they were otherwise quiet for the reading of God's Word.

Pearl passed out sheets of paper. A snicker sounded, and she knew it was one of the Rome boys. Thomas and Timothy. Tall, yet skinny, with dark hair that needed a good combing, they were identical twins and she wondered how she'd ever keep them apart. She was also certain they had traded seats when her back was turned. She decided to ignore it for now.

"I want every one to either write a story or draw a picture this morning—"

"I can't write," interrupted Tim, or was it Tom?

"It's to be in essay form." Pearl began, ignoring his comment as she handed out pencils and paper. "Write what you like about school. Or perhaps you want to tell me what you did this summer."

"I'd like it better if we had a pretty teacher," said Carl, the boy at the last desk. His face was dirty, his clothes soiled and ragged. He was bigger than the twins and wore a defiant look.

The words stung, but Pearl thought of the adage, and recited it.

"'If wishes were horses, beggars would ride.'"

Carl shuffled his feet. "That's a dumb saying."

"Please, start writing."

The younger children who could not write were to draw a picture. They would work on writing numbers and letters soon. There was more commotion in the back.

"I want to see you writing. Now." Pearl walked between the desks.

"If you don't do it now, you will stay after school to finish."

The boys groaned, then Thomas spoke up. "I don't ever have to stay after school. My father won't hear of it."

"Then I'll think of something you can do here. I expect you to do the lessons. You cannot be excused just because your father is head of the school board."

His face turned bright red. Pearl had not been exposed to hatred, but she saw it flash in his eyes. She shivered. She must outsmart him and the others who stared at her a daring way, but how? It was imperative to maintain control. To lose the upper hand meant that everything would fall apart.

Pearl admired some of the drawings, then looked at Mary Alice's full-page essay. She seemed so sweet, so wanting to please, but there was a sad look on her face and Pearl couldn't imagine how it must be to lose one's mother.

"Essays are dumb," Carl said grumbling. "I definitely don't like this lesson."

"Teachers are stupid," Timothy added. "And ugly," another voice said under his breath. "Why do you suppose she isn't married?" hissed a third. Pearl heard the stinging words, but pretended she had not. It was better to ignore some things. Soon it quieted down, but she sensed she hadn't heard the end of it.

Pearl let the students take a longer recess, watching the boys play tag while the girls played hopscotch. She knew they all needed the exercise, but especially the older boys who were used to working in the fields, not sitting at a desk all day. Then it was math and reading in the afternoon.

As the afternoon sun came in the west window, she allowed each to get a drink of water, though the boys didn't want to settle down after that. Pearl felt a sinking sensation. There was trouble ahead; she sensed it with her very being. Discipline could be a major problem. What would she do? How could she make the older ones understand the importance of learning? She thought of the books her teacher had read each day. Every student had looked forward to that time. Could she try that here? But what of Mr. Rome's admoniton that there would be no reading of books?

Pearl was thankful when she heard the horses clip-clopping outside and glanced at her watch. Three-thirty. Her first day of school was over. And, somehow, she had lived through it. One day down and forty school days to go until the Christmas holidays, when she could go home. Home. How far away it seemed. How long ago it seemed. Yet she knew she would make it, for God was on her side. He would help her through.

three

Judson Rome assisted Pearl up front while Mary Alice climbed into the back of the buggy.

"I trust the day went well."

Pearl was't sure what Mr. Rome wanted to hear. The Rome twins had continued to test her. Big boys of eleven, they had to be told twice to open their books, twice to get their feet under the desk and not to talk unless spoken to. Two other boys, John Mac and Carl were even bigger, with louder mouths. The smaller children had been a joy, especially Mary Alice Rome. Pearl had watched her as she bent over her work and painstakingly wrote her alphabet, then her numbers. She so wanted to please. If only the boys cooperated half as well.

"I know everyone's name," Pearl finally said.

Mary Alice chatted about her essay and how she could now add and subtract. Pearl smiled. Maybe the boys didn't like her, but Mary Alice did, and it helped her feelings of despair.

"And how did your brothers do?" Judson asked.

"They don't like writing," she said, her voice dropping.

Pearl glanced at Judson sideways, hoping he would let the matter drop. She just wanted to go home, get into her comfortable muslin, and talk to Nina while

26

they prepared dinner.

At last Judson pulled into the yard and Pearl lighted from the buggy and hurried inside, stopping long enough to wave once more at Mary Alice.

"Dinner will be ready in thirty minutes," called Nina.

"I'll help in a bit," Pearl called back from her bedroom space, slipping the yellow dress down past her narrow hips.

"No need. Not tonight. After one look at thee, I know thee needs complete silence and rest."

"Do you think I'll be able to teach the children?" Pearl asked a few minutes later, as she set a plate of sliced bread on the table.

"Of course thee will." Nina smiled as she looked at Pearl. "Here I am just one year ahead of you, but I feel so much older."

"That's because you're married."

"And going to have a baby," Nina added.

John came in and washed up at the basin. He was quiet, but a good man. One knew that after seeing his broad face and the look of compassion in his eyes. Pearl was lucky to be here in this home where her friends served God and loved him above all.

The meal was pleasant, but Pearl kept thinking of how it would be back at Ben's. Emily waiting with the food keeping hot in the warmer on top of the new stove Ben had ordered from the Sears & Roebuck catalog. Sarah, setting the table, or rocking baby Clifford should he be fussy. The sounds of the horses drawing up out front, then around to the side where Ben would give them their hay for the night. And Paul. Washing up out back, coming in filling the doorway with his broad shoulders, the smile on his face as he seemed to seek her out. Of course it was her imagination as Paul liked everyone and if he had eyes for someone, it was Nancy Whitfield. How could Pearl even dare think that a man as handsome as Paul could look at plain, tall Pearl?

"Why is thee smiling?" Nina asked as she passed the bowl of mashed potatoes.

"Oh. Was I?" Pearl felt her cheeks flush. "I expect I was just thinking about home and how many there'd be around the table."

She quickly added that though she missed her family, she was as proud and happy to be here in this home, eating with these friends who had made room for her.

"Thee has a right nice family, all right," Nina said. "I miss all our friends in Portland." Then seeing the look on her husband's face, she added, "But God has been good to us here. The land is good for growing and we're going to add on another ten acres soon."

John wiped his mouth with his napkin. "Yes, God has certainly attended to our needs."

Pearl wondered if God would hear her prayer tonight when she asked for help with school.

"Hear thee has some big, mean boys in the schoolroom," John said then.

Pearl nodded and looked at her hands. They were knotting in her lap. "They don't want to be there. Boys that age would rather be out in the fields, working."

John pushed back his chair. "I didn't go beyond sixth grade, Miss Pearl. I wonder if we're doing the right thing—pushing this education thing on our young boys.

Seems it might be okay for the womenfolk, but boys need to be busy at hard labor."

Pearl nodded, but knew she had to say her feelings on the subject, just as she'd spoken freely and openly with Judson Rome.

"That might be true, John, but doesn't thee ever wish for more learning? Don't you wish you had stayed in school longer?"

John hesitated, his hand on his hat as he stood by the door. "No, can't rightly say that I do. I like things just the way they are. And now if you ladies will excuse me, I got to see to my chores."

Long after the dishes were done, bread mixed and put to rise on the back of the stove, and after John had come back inside, Pearl walked out across the barren front yard. It needed some color, not just plain, brown dirt, hard-packed from summer's heat and from the wagon rolling over it. She missed the green grass, the roses Emily grew in front of the house, the other flowers that came up by the porch. If only she had some flower seeds. Why hadn't she thought of that before leaving Portland?

Pearl's long, gray skirt swept across the parched ground as she gazed into the sky. Soon it would be dark and clear. She thought of the numerous times she and Paul had watched as dusk came, then the growing darkness and the sky overflowing with stars. She remembered the time they had tried to count the stars— an impossible task. Later they had eaten pieces of Pearl's apple pie and tall glasses of water, then Paul had left to go out back where he slept, and she and climbed the stairs to the room she shared with Sarah.

A knot rose in her throat. How dearly she loved her mother. How much she wanted to go to her now and tell her about the boys, ask her advice in how to handle them. Maybe she wasn't old enough to teach. Maybe she wasn't meant to be a teacher. How did one ever really know? How could she still her beating heart when she thought of Paul? How could she know what God intended for her to do with her life? Was it right to pray for a husband, a family, when that might not be God's intent for her? "Thy will be done, Lord. Thy will be done," she prayed aloud.

Pearl walked to the end of the pasture and laughed when the mare, Missy, trotted over. She patted her side, then her head. "Are you as lonely as I am?" she said, nuzzling her close.

She'd always preferred familiar things; had dreaded leaving the farm in Iowa when she and Sarah had come out to Oregon to live with Ben. Their first house in Oregon City had had several acres and Pearl had planted a garden. But that spring was wetter than usual and the seeds had rotted.

"It isn't like Iowa," Ben explained when Pearl had all but cried over her ruined beans and tomatoes. "Spring comes much later here, but you can harvest into fall. Things don't die on the vine as they did back home."

Pearl planted seeds again and they harvested a few onions, carrots and beans, then she and Sarah moved to the big house on Foster Road—the house Ben built for Emily. And it was good they had done so as Sarah became more ill with each passing month. She couldn't be left alone when Pearl went to help Emily out before Baby Isobelle was born. Doctors were closer in Portland, too, so Sarah could get medicine for the cough that lingered on.

It was growing late and Pearl wanted to go over her lessons before bedtime. After one more call to Missy, she turned and walked back to the house. Just as she rounded the corner, she saw the familiar team of horses trotting up the road. Her heart sank. Judson Rome. What was he doing here?

Pearl tucked a few loose strands of hair behind her ear, knowing she should look her best at all times. Then she held her breath as Judson hopped down and strode over.

Dressed in a white shirt and dark tie, he had slicked his hair back from the sides of his face. Smiling, he approached her.

"I've come calling on you, Miss Galloway. I know it isn't proper to be courted without the presence of a chaperone, but the Colvilles are nearby. Keep in mind," and he licked his lips, "that I'm the chairman of the school board, so whatever I say goes."

Pearl looked skyward and asked for help. "Perhaps you've come calling on me, Mr. Rome, but I didn't hear myself saying it was okay."

"Well, I just assumed—"

"Mr. Rome, I came here to teach, not to get married. You know that one cannot be married and still be a teacher." She shot him a quizzical look. "I do believe you remember the set of rules you gave me the day I arrived?"

Judson bristled. "Yes, well, that's my point exactly.

My children need a mother far more than this community needs a teacher. I expect you need to be occupied,
plus have enough funds to take care of yourself, so my
solution is the best one for both of us!"

Pearl felt caught. Trapped. What could she say next?
How could she even consider being called on by this
man when she found him so disreputable? So lacking
in manners and simple courtesy?

"If and when I should want to be called on, Mr.
Rome, I think I'll be the one deciding who that might
be. Thank you for stopping by."

He sputtered, exclaiming he'd see her in the morning,
as she hurried off inside the house. So that was the real
reason she was asked to come. It wasn't to teach, but to
marry Mr. Judson Rome, to provide a home for him, to
cook for the family and to mother his children. She
could have taken Mary Alice under her wing in a
moment, but not the twins. They needed discipline, and
she knew she wasn't capable of handling them. They
also needed a father who cared, but somehow she
thought that Judson Rome cared for nobody but himself.

Pearl watched while the team of horses left in a cloud
of dust, then headed back to the house.

Nina was setting out bowls for the next morning's
breakfast and glanced up with a puzzled look.

"I see Mr. Rome came calling on thee."

"He did."

"And what did thee talk about?"

"That I came to teach, not to be courted."

"Thee probably shouldn't have refused Judson," Nina

said as she poured Pearl a cup of coffee.

"I know." Pearl set the cup down. "I don't know why I said what I did, but I honestly cannot bear to think of him calling on me."

"He has a lot of influence in this town."

"I realize that, Nina. Oh, how I realize it."

"He was the one who said we needed a school-teacher."

"Yes, he told me." Pearl shivered and drew her shawl closer.

"He could see to it that thee was replaced by another teacher."

"And you think he will?"

Nina nodded. "I think thee needs to pray about it."

"Then let's pray that God's will be done and let it rest at that."

Later Pearl set out her dark calico, and the lessons for tomorrow. She lit the lamp and sat at the table, penning a note to Emily.

Dear Emily, and to anyone else who might be interested, I arrived. The schoolhouse is new. There's a beautiful little stove in it.

I have sixteen pupils and so far Mary Alice is my favorite one, though I realize that teachers should not have pets.

I miss everyone there. I just wish I could come home to see you all. Baby Clifford. I want to hold him close and nuzzle his soft cheek next to mine. Emily, to just chat with you. Mama, to ask advice, to hear tell that I've

*made the right decision by coming here. Ben
who is such a dear brother, and Paul who likes
to gaze at the stars on a warm summer
evening.*

She signed off, wondering if it was all right that
she'd included Paul. Would he even read the letter?
Surely he didn't care, but how could she talk about
everyone else and leave him out?

She blew out the light and crawled under the sheet. It
was too warm for covers, but before dawn, she'd pull
the heavy quilt up under her chin. By morning it would
be cool and she would ride to school with the sun just
coming up over the eastern hill, filling the sky with its
brilliance.

Pearl prayed for wisdom, and several verses came to
mind: "God is love." "God cares for you." She believed
it. She held God's Word tight to her chest. He knew
what was best for her. Tomorrow was another day, and
that thought made her remember another favorite
Psalm: "Trust in the Lord thy God with all thy heart,
soul and strength and he shall direct thy paths."

Pearl thought of Paul and how he had not accepted
God as his maker, his redeemer, but Paul was God's
creation. He would always be God's creation. Nothing
Paul did or said, or didn't do or say could change
things. Still, Pearl thought Paul did care, did believe in
God; he just didn't know it yet.

When sleep didn't come, she remembered one hot
summer afternoon, the day of the water fight. . . .

The evening meal had been prepared and two of

Pearl's apple pies lay cooling on the counter. Pearl had also fed the chickens, changed Clifford's diaper and rocked him to sleep, all the while telling him he was a very special baby, even if he was a trifle spoiled. He was teething and crankier than usual. Emily and Sarah were taking naps. Paul would have gone with Ben to work on one of the new homes across the river, but he was learning to plaster and had stayed home to perfect his craft. He'd chosen a wall just outside the kitchen steps to practice on.

First Paul mixed the plaster until it was the right consistency, then he took the trowel and smeared a large amount on the wall, using long, swirling motions. He'd stand back, survey his work, then smile if he was pleased. If not, he'd take it off, dumping it back into the trough, add a little water or cement, and start all over again. Ben had said this was the best way to learn.

Just as Paul started to throw the mixture back in, Pearl came around the corner. Startled, he slipped and fell into the trough. It was his look of surprise that made Pearl laugh more than anything. She knew she shouldn't laugh, but she couldn't help it.

"If you aren't a sight, Paul Drake!" she screeched.

At first Paul glared, but the more Pearl laughed, the more he saw humor in the situation. Besides, one could hardly keep a straight face when Pearl laughed.

"It isn't funny," he said wiping the white, wet stuff from his leg and foot.

"I wish I had a camera," she said between laughs.

"Well, I'm glad you don't." He turned and walked over to a bucket of water and dipped his hand in.

She stood at the corner of the house, watching and attempting to stifle her giggles as he began washing off the plaster. Suddenly, he threw a whole dipper of water on her, and another. Soon the front of the old navy blue calico was soaked, her hair had slipped out of the ribbon and hung in wet streaks about her face. Pearl stared in disbelief.

"Pearl—Gem—I don't know what came over me—" he began.

In answer, she laughed as she shook her dress out. "Just you wait," she cried, laughing even harder. Then she threw a dipperful on him and chased him around the side of the house.

He caught her hands and held her so she couldn't move. Suddenly, Pearl stopped struggling and stared. As their eyes locked, her heart beat faster. It was almost as if the world stood still, and Pearl was to wonder later what might have happened if Emily hadn't called out then.

She stood in the doorway, holding Clifford close. "I heard laughter and wondered—" She looked from Pearl to Paul, and then started laughing. The baby who had not yet learned to laugh, looked at his mother and then his tiny voice joined in the melee.

"His first laugh!" Pearl cried out. And then she flipped water from her fingers onto his face. He laughed even harder.

"If you two don't look a sight! You'd better both get washed up."

Pearl's shoes squeaked as she went up the stairs. She changed into her oldest muslin, pulled her hair back into a knot, foregoing her usual braid. She tried to put

Paul out of her mind, the way he had looked at her, but the thought kept coming back, even later as she mashed potatoes for dinner.

Nobody spoke of the plaster incident again, but Pearl knew she would never forget that afternoon and the way they had looked at each other.

The sound of the wind whistling around the sides of the small house finally drew Pearl into a dreamless sleep. . . .

four

In the two weeks that followed, Judson Rome persisted in his quest to court Pearl. He'd asked her to go buggy riding, to accompany him to a barn dance, and to attend his church. Pearl had declined all offers. She knew there would be no turning back if she once said yes. But Judson was stubborn, and not one to give up easily.

"Every woman has something she will say yes to," he said one afternoon after school as they drove over the road to the Colville's.

"I prefer teaching," Pearl said for what she knew must be the hundredth time.

"We shall see."

"He seems to think it makes everything all right because he owns a vast acreage and large house, that I should be happy to agree to his proposal of marriage," Pearl lamented to Nina as she tore off the outer wrappings of a package that had arrived from Portland. She could hardly wait to see what Emily had sent.

"Perhaps he will continue in an effort to wear thee down. Or, he might find a way to rid thee of thy teaching position. And the boys have been difficult," Nina added.

Pearl nodded as she withdrew the contents from the cardboard box. "Believe me, I have considered the proposal, but wish it were from a different person."

Pencils, paper, string, glue, and best of all three books. One was *The Night Before Christmas* by Clement C. Moore, and the other two were *Robinson Crusoe* and *Gulliver's Travels.*

Pearl clutched the books close to her bosom. "*Robinson Crusoe* is the first book I shall read. It's the one thing that might keep the older boys interested in coming to school. Some good with the difficult ones."

"And the paints?" Nina asked.

"Later, for Christmas."

Pearl would teach math in the morning, read a chapter, followed by English and recess. Afternoons they'd practice penmanship, something the boys detested. Pearl also planned a brief history lesson starting today.

Judson Rome arrived the following morning, after insisting that it was only proper that he continue to pick her up to and from school. Pearl continued dreading the trip, but it did no good, so she prayed for patience with this man. He held his hand out to assist her, and she took it be grudgingly.

"What's in the box?" he asked, his eyes narrowing.

"School supplies."

"Did we not furnish you with paper and pencils?"

"Yes, but this is extra. Drawing paper and paints and—" She hesitated, realizing she dare not mention the reading books.

Besides, they were good reading books. Hadn't her teacher read them to her at school in Portland?

"Don't take up time with frivolous pursuits," Judson said then.

"It is for days when it rains too much to go outside."

"The children need to go outside." He watched her, but Pearl wouldn't look his way. "Rain never hurt anyone."

"A fine morning it is," Pearl declared, in an effort to change the subject. Actually, it would be a fine morning once she arrived at school. Though fall mornings were cool, and often rainy, the sun was beaming today and its warmth filled Pearl with promise. Promise of a better day than what yesterday had been. If only she could reach the boys by reading *Robinson Crusoe*.

"I've seen better," Judson finally grumped. "Why are you so cheerful?"

Pearl smiled. "I'm always cheerful in the morning, thanking the Lord for yet another day to celebrate life."

Judson grunted again. "Don't start preaching. I've had enough preaching to last a lifetime."

Seems not much of it rubbed off on you, Pearl longed to say, but she saw no need to get Judson's anger riled up and ruin her perfect day. There'd be time for that later when the boys arrived all full of pep and arguments.

"I been meaning to talk to you about something, Miss Galloway. Mary Alice tells me the boys have been giving you a hard time."

"Yes, there are four of them who have a problem settling down."

A sudden scowl crossed his broad face. "My boys can be a bit rambunctious at times—"

"Calling the teacher names goes beyond being rambunctious," Pearl cut in. "I would like—with your permission of course—to keep them after school. They can write extra sentences or read a chapter in the history book—"

"Absolutely not! You'll not single out my sons just because you don't have control of the class."

"And I might have control if I was allowed some means of discipline."

"They're good boys," Judson retorted. "A gentle reminder should work nicely."

"Gentle?" Pearl cried. "Those boys don't know the meaning of the word." She half expected Mary Alice to comment from the backseat, but she knew when to keep quiet and this was one of those times. What the boys needed was a sound thrashing. Pearl, being a Quaker, was opposed to violence, yet wondered if there couldn't be an exception to the rule.

"Ignore their capers," Judson said then. "The more air you give a flame, the higher it goes."

Pearl had one last thing to try and she'd begin today. Surely they would obey as they would want her to keep reading the story.

If she didn't receive respect soon, she would have to quit, though she never considered herself a quitter. She thought of Mama's saying again: "Quitters never win, and winners never quit."

She prayed nightly and knew Emily, Ben and Sarah prayed, as well as Nina and John, but she had to find the answers herself, and these books were the answer.

"If a teacher doesn't have control of her class, perhaps there is something wrong with her method of teaching," Judson said then, a smirk on his face.

Pearl stared straight ahead, saying nothing.

"I hope you won't expect a good recommendation, in the event you quit."

"Not that I would expect one."

"I trust you'll continue on until Christmas break—maybe winter break?"

"Of course." Pearl realized now what he was doing—setting her up for failure so she'd be forced into quitting then agreeing to marry him. He thought she'd be too ashamed to return home to admit her failure.

Judson didn't help her down from the buggy, which Pearl was thankful for. She adjusted her bonnet and stepped over a huge mud puddle by the front door and entered the building. One student had arrived. It was Cora Gentry.

"Cora, did you come alone?"

"Yes, Miss Galloway."

"Why didn't you wait for your brother?"

Her small face looked so serious.

"Cora, what is it? You're absolutely trembling."

"It's the boys. I had to come early to tell you."

"The boys?" She removed her bonnet and hung it on a nail in the corner. Her gloves were placed on the shelf below the hat. She turned to look at the pinched face of her next-to-youngest pupil. "What boys are you referring to?" Pearl walked over to Cora and held the small, trembling hands.

"They were a talking yesterday, Miss Galloway. I overheard them when they thought I was playing during recess."

"And what did you hear?"

"They are going to put a snake in the desk drawer when we're out for recess. They want to scare you off."

Pearl shuddered for the second time that morning. A snake. Of all God's creatures she feared snakes the most. Did the boys know that, or were they making a good guess?

She looked at Cora and wanted to take the child into her arms. She decided to do that very thing, favoritism or not. Cora, like Mary Alice had no mother. Her brother, Carl, just like the twins, demanded attention and got it by naughty behavior.

"Cora, it was a brave thing you did, coming to tell me this. I'll figure out a way to surprise them back."

The thin shoulders seemed to rise under the thin cotton dress as she smiled. "I like you Miss Galloway. Better than anyone I know."

"And I like you very much, too."

"You won't tell on me, will you?"

Pearl held her tighter. "Of course I won't, Cora. I'm good at keeping secrets."

Cora smiled and hugged Pearl back. "I wish you were my mother," she said before sitting back down.

Pearl felt her heart pound. If only she could reach the boys. Well today she would try it. Since she was quitting at the end of the term anyway, why not go ahead and start reading *Robinson Crusoe*. If the boys weren't interested in a shipwrecked sailor on a deserted island, she doubted they'd ever be interested in reading or literature of any kind.

The sounds of horses drew up outside and soon the schoolhouse was full of boys and voices and talking.

Pearl let them talk as they shuffled to their seats. It was ten minutes before class began. She'd ask Cora to lead the flag salute this morning.

Later as Pearl looked out over the desks and a few leering faces, she decided to go with her plan. After Scripture, she would begin chapter one of *Robinson Crusoe*. Then, when she had them hooked, she would say it was time to write their numbers. Two more pages would be read if all work was completed and handed in.

The book was welcomed. There were no disturbing voices or feet shuffling as even the older boys leaned on their hands and listened. Once in a while Pearl would stop and ask a question about what they would do in that situation. Nobody seemed to know and they would beg her to read on so they could find out. When she reached the end of the first chapter, she found the bookmark and closed the book. At first there was silence, then every one began talking at once.

"You can't stop there," Timothy said, being the first to speak out. "We have to know what he did."

"We have other things we must do."

"But we gotta know what happens," Timothy insisted.

"There will be more chapters later on if you do your work promptly."

There were groans, but the boys took out their tablets and pens.

After recess, Pearl watched out of the corner of her eye from the edge of the play area. She thought she saw two boys slip back into the school building, but she couldn't be positive.

When she rang the small silver bell to mark the end of recess, Pearl was ready and waiting. After everyone found their seats, she asked them to open their reading books.

"Kenny," she called out. "My desk drawer seems to be sticking. Could you come open it for me?"

Kenny, a second-grader, not in on the trick, shuffled up to the front of the class. He had trouble learning, but he showed Pearl respect.

"No! Wait!" Thomas called from the back of the room. "I'll do it!

"I think Kenny is capable," Pearl said.

"But I'm more capable," Thomas insisted, making his way to the front of the room.

"Very well, then." Pearl stood back and closed her eyes, not wanting to see a snake in any shape or form, no matter who had it or what it was doing.

Thomas opened the door and Pearl saw movement out of the corner of her eye. She held her mouth closed tightly, willing herself not to scream.

Thomas shook his head, as if bewildered and held the snake in his large hand. "Gosh, Miss Galloway, there seems to be a snake here. I wonder how on earth it got here?"

Pearl gasped, then smiled. "My goodness, yes, I wonder how."

Thomas disappeared out the door and Pearl heard some muted whispers from the back of the room. Well, they would plan on something else. She was sure she hadn't heard the end of the snake incident.

And Cora, rewarded for her role of snitching, arrived

the next morning with a welt on her leg, and red-rimmed eyes. Since everyone had arrived, Pearl could not ask what had happened, but she suspected Carl had given her a whipping. How dare he! How could she make sure her students were not beaten by older siblings?

That afternoon Judson Rome asked about the snake incident. "I hear tell you had a snake in the schoolroom yesterday."

"Yes, well, it got in the desk drawer somehow, but I think the problem's been resolved."

"Resolved? And how could that be?"

"The offending pupils who had something to do with that are going to chop some wood for the stove so they'll have heat come winter."

Judson looked puzzled. "And you know who these offending pupils are?"

Pearl smiled and looked straight ahead. "I do."

"It ain't either of my boys."

Pearl still wouldn't look him in the eye. "That's for me to know and for you to find out, Mr. Rome."

"You ain't saying, because you don't know."

"Oh, I know all right. Never fear about that—"

"Someone snitched then."

"You might call it that."

"That isn't fair play to tattle like that and you know it."

"Nor is it fair to try to harm the schoolteacher."

Judson hit the reins and his team reared. "Like I said before, perhaps you aren't fit to teach school, Miss Galloway."

And, perhaps you, sir, aren't fit to be a father, Pearl longed to say, but kept the words tight inside her. Judson Rome appeared on the outside to be a law-abiding, God-fearing citizen of his community, but he was a bully. Mean. Conniving. He stepped on toes, and if he didn't get his way, he'd retaliate in some way. Either everyone did not know what he was doing, or they chose to look the other way in case they might be the target for his abuse. She did not want to be part of such actions and might even tell him so one day.

In the meantime, she was doing the one thing he had forbidden her to do: read a book to her students. The boys did not tell on her because they were too interested in the story and wanted to find out what happened. Yes, she had a hold on them, at least for now. After *Robinson Crusoe*, she would read another. Emily's bookshelves hosted several volumes. She might write to see if Emily could send her Elsie Dinsmore books. She knew Mary Ann and Cora would like to read them. All her pupils could read well now and Pearl was proud of her first class, even if there were other problems. Nothing ever ran completely smoothly. Life just wasn't that way.

five

Paul Michael Drake stood at the mirror, trimming the beginning of a beard. It was straggly at best and thin in spots, and he wondered why he kept trying to grow it. His hair, the color of sand, was thick and long. It was time for a cut, but there was no rush. Nobody to impress now that Pearl was gone. Blue eyes stared back at him from the mirror and he wondered what Pearl was doing this very minute.

Paul had never realized he would miss Pearl so much. She was just one of the family. They were just friends and one missed their friends, but his feelings went deeper than that. The first inkling he'd had was after a water fight one afternoon. She'd looked into his eyes with such intensity, it had unnerved him. Now he found himself thinking about her constantly, wondering what she'd say about this, think about that. He hadn't shared his thoughts with anyone, though he expected Ben knew—after their conversation yesterday on the way home from work.

"Sure seems quiet with Pearl gone, doesn't it," Ben had said.

It wasn't a question, but more of a statement.

Paul nodded. "And it isn't that she talks that much."

"No," Ben said in agreement. "Pearl's always been quiet. Well, perhaps not as quiet as Emily, but quieter than the rest of us. Of course then there's Jesse. Jesse can out-talk every one of us Galloways."

Paul turned and stared at his brother-in-law. Ben rarely spoke of Jesse, and Emily all but refused to allow his name be mentioned in her presence. He knew that Jesse, the oldest of the Galloways had broken many hearts, but it was Kate's heart that Emily remembered, for Kate had nearly married Jesse, but he had run off and nobody had heard from him now for well over a year.

"I knew someone in California like that," Paul said. "He worked for us one summer. That's after Pa died and Ma needed some stuff done around the place. He said he could do anything she needed fixing and wouldn't charge much."

Ben let the reins go slack. "So? Did he do what he said he could do?"

"Nope! Ran off with the shed half built. We all had to finish the job and Ma was right out there, pounding nails, too."

"Jesse never did anything like hold a hammer," Ben said. "He's a genteel man. One who can't get his hands dirty."

"Never held a hammer?" Paul repeated.

"Don't rightly think so."

Paul eased back against the seat. "Strange how some people see things differently. How they don't see things like the rest of us do. Like being honest."

"Or worshiping God," Ben said.

Paul looked away. He didn't like to get on the subject of God. It wasn't that he didn't believe, because maybe he did, just a bit. But he couldn't say he rightfully belonged to God, either. Not like the others spoke of. Maybe he just had to be shown, to see proof. Yes, that was it. He needed proof.

"I don't exactly worship God, Ben, but I'm a good person, or at least I like to think so."

Ben nodded. "Yeah. A lot of people think that works is what makes you belong, but it isn't. It's faith and believing."

"Well, then, guess I am just a plain ole heathen." He turned and caught Ben's arm. "Not that you have to go tellin' Emily that. Don't know what she'd do to me if she heard how I felt about religion and God and such."

Ben smiled. "Your secret's safe with me, Paul. I think you're just one of those people who don't exactly believe, but don't rightly disbelieve, either."

"I think it's important to Pearl, too." The minute Paul had said the words, he wondered why he had even thought of her. It made him sound as if he had serious thoughts about Pearl and he didn't. Or he didn't think he did. Not exactly, that is.

Or did he?

Long after the two men arrived home, greeted Sarah and Emily, and after Paul played with his nephew and they sat down to dinner, thoughts of Pearl kept hitting him. He didn't want to think about her. He knew she didn't think of him as anything more than brother. But her face kept getting in the way. It got in the way of his gazing at the jet black sky and intruded on his thoughts when he went to bed and lay propped up with arms under his head. He wondered how Pearl was faring this very moment. Wondered how she was getting along in a strange place, teaching children. At least she had friends to board with. Yet, he found himself counting the days until Christmas when he knew she'd be home. Even if only for a month or so, she'd be here and they'd talk.

Nancy Whitfield came to mind. Pretty and tiny, Nancy had golden curls and a pair of the bluest eyes he'd ever seen. Her smile always seemed directed at him, but try as he might, he couldn't seem to smile back.

She sat across the aisle during church, talked to him after the meeting, asked for a ride once when her father had to leave early. He remembered taking her; he had an old team of horses and a rickety wagon, but she didn't seem to notice, or if she did, she didn't mind.

"I just think our church is so special, don't you, Paul?"

Then without waiting for an answer, she bubbled on, "and I like our new minister."

Pastor Luke Morrison and his wife, Kate, had started a new church down south in the valley and Paul missed his friends.

"I don't think anyone could ever take Pastor Luke's place," Paul started to say, but Nancy cut him right off and went trilling off on how the area was growing, how she hoped to move, to have a home someday a bit closer to town.

"Don't you just love it in Oregon? So much is happening. I mean it's better than California—" And again before he could answer, she was talking about

California and how people were going there because of the weather and growing seasons, but how much better Oregon was in spite of the rain.

"Do you agree? Paul?" She raised puzzled eyes in his direction.

"Agree?" he said, when he realized she was waiting for his answer. "What am I supposed to agree to? That California is not a good place to live, or that Oregon is growing, or that you prefer living in town to the country?" Or had she said something else that he'd missed entirely? He wasn't good with small talk, and sometimes he just liked the silence. In fact, preferred it.

Her face flushed bright red. "Oh! I've done it again, haven't I?" And then before he could answer, she went on exclaiming how her own mother said she never let people get a word in edgewise.

"And that's true, isn't it, Paul? Oh, you needn't answer, for I know it is. I truly do."

Paul felt relief when the Whitfield farm came into sight.

"Won't you come in for a glass of buttermilk and some cookies? I made them yesterday—they have oats and raisins and walnuts. They're called Poor Man's Cookies, though heavens know we're not poor!"

Paul shook his head. "Thanks, but I have to get back to help Ben."

"What? Work on the Lord's Day? Surely you can't mean you work on Sunday." He knew he would be in for another long dissertation so he excused himself, tipped his hat, and turned the horse around before she could say anything more. Or at least say anything he could hear.

"Pearl wasn't like that at all." He was talking to the wind and occasionally, the horse turned his head just a little as if he was listening.

"You heard me," Paul said. "Pearl gives a guy a chance to answer. She gives the air a minute to settle down and around a person. Nancy keeps it moving, shuffling it up with her endless chatter."

Paul hit the reins and the horse started off in a gallop. No, there wasn't work to be done. He had said that, not thinking how it might sound to Nancy. The only work they would do was sit and read in the parlour or sit on the front porch and watch the traffic go by. Not that much happened on Sundays. He might play with Clifford, or rock him to sleep if Emily needed a moment's rest or Sarah was too ill to help out.

The rest of the journey was spent thinking about Pearl, remembering how she'd made him a special apple tart to take to work. She packed his sandwiches, putting in an extra one on days when she knew he had extra work. She was one of the nicest, sweetest girls he had ever known. But, no, he knew she thought of him as a brother. Pearl wanted to teach school besides. And when you taught, you definitely could not marry or have a family. The schoolchildren were a teacher's family. No, Pearl would not think of him twice as a possible husband. And it was just as well. Paul couldn't believe as she did. Pearl would need a religious person, just as Ben was suitable for Emily. And Kate for Luke. Though Paul had heard that Kate had not always believed. Sudden inspiration hit. Perhaps he needed to talk to Kate. It just might be a good idea.

It was late, very dark and the night's chill had settled around the porch when Paul finally tiptoed off to bed. But try as he might, his thoughts were on Pearl with the shy smile, the brown hair she wore in long, coiled braids, the way her tall body looked when she was dressed up for church, the way she had looked the morning before leaving on the train.

He'd wanted to take her to the station, but Ben had offered, and Sarah went along to wish her youngest child blessings and to send her off with a hearty farewell.

Before they left, Paul had wanted to reach up and give Pearl a light kiss on the cheek. Surely she wouldn't have minded, but it was probably just as well that he had not done so.

Paul thought of other things that night. His family. The way they followed the crops from spring to fall. Winter found them further south where vegetables grew abundantly in the middle of winter. Actually, winter never came to the Imperial Valley.

He never liked the moving, and remembered Pa, more than once, standing at the end of his row, glaring, threatening him if he stopped for even a moment to glance around. You had to keep busy. The more you picked, the more money you made and the nicer house the family could buy when they moved further north.

Paul had gone to school through sixth grade. His father took him out then because he was lean and tall for his age, and broad-shouldered. People thought he was much older than he was.

"You don't need to go to school, anyway. Larnin's for sissies."

It was for that reason Paul felt he was no match for Pearl. She had taken the test enabling her to teach to elementary children. She was smart. She knew a lot of things Paul didn't know. Of course he could stucco the whole outside of a house, plaster the rooms inside, and as she told him more than once she had no idea of how to do that.

"You are smart in your own way, Paul," Pearl had said one night when they sat on the porch steps watching a sky full of stars. "Each of us is smart in his own way."

Pearl never said an unkind thing about anyone. She refused to say anything about Jesse even. "There's good in all people. We just have to look harder for it in some," she'd said.

Paul wished he could believe that. He wished he could carve out of wood as Ben did. Then he'd carve an animal for Pearl, and give it to her at Christmas when she came home. But he couldn't. He'd tried. He thought about the books Emily read. He'd tried to read some, but most of the words were complicated. At least Emily had finished school. He should tell Emily that sometime when she mentioned how much she missed growing up with her family.

He picked up the small notebook Emily had given him. It was supposed to be for writing down his thoughts. Well, he couldn't do that. What thoughts?

Pearl had sent him a short note when she wrote Emily to ask for school supplies. Paul unfolded the page and stared at the handwriting.

My Friend, Paul:

How are you? Did you finish the Creighton
house in Moreland? Do you give Clifford a hug
each morning and each night for me? Please
know that my thoughts and prayers are with
you.

I count the days until Christmas. . . .

As Ever,
Gem

Paul read the letter twice, then refolded it and stuck it
under his pillow. He liked keeping it there. It was as if
Pearl were close by, part of him, feeling his heartbeat
as he slept. . . .

Paul opened the small tablet and picked up a pencil
and wrote her name at the top of the page.

Pearl:

I miss you, I do.
I wonder if you miss me half as much.
Christmas will be here soon, and I wish
you could stay and not go back to teach. . . .

It didn't say much, but he'd give it to her at Christmas.
Knowing Pearl, she'd appreciate it.

He wrote a few more lines, but they sounded silly. He
scribbled through the words. The only thing he could
do was plaster a house. A sudden thought hit. What if
he designed one? A special house with Pearl in mind. It
would need a big kitchen because she liked to cook and
bake. He'd order one of those new stoves from the

Sears catalog. It would be all shiny with lots of chrome, so you could see your face in it. and he'd rent one of those new-fangled irons from PGE. If you liked it, after a month's trial, you could buy it for four dollars. Wouldn't Pearl like ironing her dresses with a spanking new electric iron?

Paul closed the tablet, slipped it under the mattress and rolled over on his side. He'd finish the letter later. No use in dreaming up things like new houses and irons. Someday there might be someone for him. Nancy Whitfield would like to think so. At least he wouldn't have to wonder about what to say next. But he couldn't begin imagining building a home for Nancy. It would never be nice enough for her. He just knew it wouldn't be. Pearl would like anything he did. Why and how did he know that?

He tried to sleep, but it was impossible. Finally, he turned on the small bed lamp again and reached for the small book on the nightstand.

Sarah had given him a Bible, insisting that everyone needed one for his very own. Paul had tried to understand the words, but some made no sense. Then he remembered what Luke had said in a sermon just before leaving Portland.

"Those of you who are new Christians need to read John and Romans. Read the Psalms and Proverbs for enlightenment." Luke had read the most important law of all from Deuteronomy: " 'Thou shalt love the Lord thy God with all thy heart, soul, might and strength.'" And the second important one came from 1 John: " 'Thou shalt love thy neighbor as thyself.'"

Paul read the underlined words. They were good laws. He knew he could and would obey these two commandments, though he did not understand their full implication. Who was his neighbor? As for love, just what sort of love did it mean? He mulled it over, closed the book and blew out the lantern.

"God, if you are there, tell me what I should do. Can Gem be part of my life, or am I going against Your wishes?"

six

Thanksgiving came, and Judson invited Pearl to spend the holiday at his house. He had a new housekeeper who would do the cooking, but she politely declined and ate turkey with Nina and John and their friends from church. She missed her family and now counted the days until school would be out for the winter break.

That Saturday Pearl began knitting socks for Christmas. Emily had sent yarn in the earlier box. She also was working on a cross-stitch pattern for Nina and John. It was a surprise. When she wasn't knitting or preparing lessons, she wrote letters. Paul had written twice now. His last letter mentioned Nancy Whitfield and Pearl's eyes unexpectedly filled with tears. She wrote back immediately:

> *Paul:*
>
> *I hope thee and Nancy will be most happy together. She is a beautiful young woman and loves the Lord very much.*
>
> *School keeps me busy. The boys are so good now. I get the wood box filled up without asking, the water is brought in from the well and Thomas insists on hanging my wraps on the nail by the door. Such a change!*
>
> *Please hug baby Clifford for me. And write again.*
>
> *Your friend,*
> *Gem*

Two weeks later Pearl received another box of paper, watercolors and brushes. She knew what they would do with the new paints—an activity all would enjoy.

Again, Judson wanted to know what was in the box, but she declined to answer.

Once the lessons were out of the way, she passed out paper and scissors for the snowflakes. "And when we finish these, we'll cut strips, paint them red and green and have paper chains to put on your trees."

"We never have a tree," Cora said.

"Well, perhaps this year you might. If you don't, you can hang the chains on the walls."

Pearl remembered the story of Emily's first Christmas with a tree and how excited she had been. She'd want one now for Clifford's first Christmas.

When the chains and snowflakes were finished, Pearl brought out the plate of taffy. She and Nina had pulled taffy, then cut it into squares and put it on one of Nina's pretty blue plates.

"After singing Christmas carols, we'll have taffy and if there's enough time I have a new story to read."

"A Christmas story?" asked Mary Alice.

"Yes, a poem, actually. It's not as beautiful as the story of Jesus's birth, but you will enjoy it, I'm sure."

"I don't want school to end," John Mac said. "I like the stories."

"Perhaps you'd like to borrow one of my books," Pearl offered.

John Mac suddenly scowled. "Pa wouldn't let me read. He says it's girl's stuff."

"I see."

"We used to think that," Timothy said then.

"Because we didn't want to study," said Thomas.

"Yeah," Carl added. "but we know it's a good idea to learn numbers and to be able to read. Just last week I read a letter for Pa, one he got from the governor of Oregon!"

"My goodness, that is wonderful," Pearl said, eager to hear what the governor had to say. "Was it good news?"

Carl whipped the letter out of his back pocket. "It was." He looked thoughtful. "My father caught a runaway horse and saved a girl's life. The governor has invited him to a special ceremony at the capitol building next Saturday to get an award."

"Carl, this is wonderful news."

"Pa said I could read the letter," Carl said, unfolding the sheet of paper. "If you want me to."

"By all means."

Carl read the words haltingly and only once did Pearl have to help, with the word *accommodations*.

"What's that long word mean?" Thomas asked, breaking in.

"It means that Carl's father will be put up, so he doesn't need to worry about going home that same night."

"I'm sure your father will enjoy going to our state's capital and collecting his award," Pearl said. "That is quite an honor."

Pearl unwrapped the dish of taffy and the kids oohed and ahhed.

"Treats after we sing and have our Christmas story."

Pearl had finished the last stanza: "'Happy Christmas to all and to all a good night'" when the door burst open.

Judson Rome stood in the doorway, eyes blazing. The children gasped.

"Miss Galloway! I've been standing outside, listening. You just now read one of those make-believe stories! And partying to boot!"

Pearl's face flushed. The room was a shambles with paper chains and snowflakes littering the desks and floors. She finally found her voice. "It's true that we're having a party, but the pupils finished their work and it is almost Christmas."

The room was so silent Pearl could almost hear her heart beat.

"Christmas is no different from any other day! I remember specifically stating that you teach the basics. This—" and he grabbed *The Night Before Christmas* and flung it across the room—" is hardly the basics."

Pearl had never been so mortified in her entire life. For a long moment she could do nothing but stand and stare. Finally she gathered her composure, walked across the room and picked up the slim volume. She examined the spine, ran her fingers over the words she loved so well and closed it gently.

She remembered the lessons she'd given the children on how to care for a book. Never bend it back. Always lay it in a flat place. Wash your hands before handling one, and absolutely, never, ever throw it on the floor. The children, eyes wide, waited to see what would happen next.

Pearl stood straight and stared at her accuser. "Mr. Rome, one can throw books and burn books, but they can never get rid of the precious words written therein.

Those we keep in our hearts."

Stunned, as if not knowing what to say, he sputtered. "The school board will have to vote on the matter, of course, but I'm afraid we have no choice but to let you go and begin our search for another teacher."

"But, Pa," Mary Ann's voice broke in. "We like Miss Galloway."

"Yes, Pa," Timothy said.

"Obviously," Judson Rome snapped, "since all you do is have fun." He picked up a chain and tore it in half. "Such frivolity! This is not what school is about. You'll be hearing from me!" Without another word, he spun on his heel and slammed out the door, shaking the windows.

There was only one more day until winter break. Pearl would still go home, as planned, then wait to hear from Judson Rome.

"My father wants to marry you," Mary Alice said during recess. "I heard him say that."

"I know, Mary Alice. If you and your brothers were all that came with the bargain, I would have accepted gladly. However, I cannot marry a man who does not like words and books and fun. I simply could not bear it."

"My mother always agreed with Papa."

"And your mother was a saint." Pearl reached over and ran fingers through the snarled curls. What she wouldn't give to mother this child. If only she could take her home. Emily would love her as her own, as would Ben and Sarah and every one else. She shook the thoughts from her mind.

Recess was over and every one came back in, blowing steamy breaths into the room. It was cold enough to snow, Pearl thought.

"Please read *The Night Before Christmas* again," they begged.

She held the book, noting the wrinkled corners. What was the harm? She no longer had a position here; she might as well read, give them some enjoyment. Heaven only knew when they might have a teacher again.

"I will read after you do one page of numbers." She passed out the arithmetic: addition for the younger ones, multiplication for the older students.

As they worked, Pearl thought about the possibility of not returning to Stayton School. She recalled one of Sarah's favorite sayings: "Things always work out for the best."

John Mac looked up from his numbers, holding his page high. "I'm all done!"

"Good, John Mac. Give everyone else a chance to finish."

"Are you really going to leave?"

"I don't know. It depends on what decision the school board makes." Pearl looked out over her classroom. "Whatever happens, I want you to remember what you have learned. I want you to do your work and cooperate with the new teacher." A funny feeling started in the pit of her stomach as Pearl realized how much she had grown to love the children.

Pearl was silent when Judson Rome came to pick her up after school.

"Perhaps I was wrong," he said as he helped her into

the buggy. "I may want you to stay, Miss Galloway."

Pearl bristled inside. "Say what you will, Mr. Rome, but I may not want to return after my winter break."

"Confound it!" He hit the reins hard. I don't understand you!"

"Nor I you."

Sudden clouds scudded across the sky then, and Pearl wondered if it meant snow. Snow didn't come often to these parts, nothing as it had in Iowa, but it did fall in November sometimes and definitely December. January was usually the worst month for snow, according to Emily, who had lived in Oregon longer than anyone else in the family. She told of the long winter when the snow lasted a week, and then ice came and stayed another week.

"There will be just one more day of school," Judson said then. "That's in the contract."

"I may go early," Pearl said. "The train leaves at 3:00 P.M. and I'd like to be on it."

Judson Rome frowned. "I can't give you full pay."

"Do as you must, Mr. Rome."

At last they were at the Colville's just as the first snowflake fell.

"It's snowing!" Mary Alice cried, coming out of her quiet lethargy.

Pearl hugged the small child, knowing she'd always remember the way her face lit up at the sight of snow.

"I will see you in the morning, Miss Galloway."

Pearl paused. "I really prefer that John take me to school tomorrow, if you don't mind."

Judson Rome sputtered in that way he had when

someone dared to cross or question him. "We shall see," he called out as Pearl hurried across the yard.

A warm fire blazed in the fireplace and Nina looked up expectantly when Pearl entered the cozy house. She hung her wraps on the nail beside the door.

"Thee looks angry."

"I am."

"I have some lemon tea. Perhaps that will help thy disposition."

"Perhaps, but don't count on it." Pearl sank into the nearest chair. "I think I've lost my teaching position, Nina."

"No. What are you saying, Pearl?"

"Judson Rome does not like my method of teaching. He wants to find another teacher." She took the cup of tea and felt its warmth. "I was never what he expected."

"But you are a good teacher."

"I know, but Judson wanted someone to marry and I wouldn't go along with the plan."

"He may change his mind before tomorrow."

"It won't do any good."

"You mean—"

"Yes, Nina. I'm sorry, because I enjoyed being here. I wanted to help with the baby. Wanted to plant flowers around the house, make new curtains. . . ."

Pearl thought of the cross-stitch pattern she was embroidering to decorate the kitchen wall. It wasn't finished, but maybe she could complete it tonight.

The wind howled around the small house and Nina looked concerned. "I thought John would be home by now."

"Perhaps I should go after him," Pearl offered.

"He's got the wagon and old Ned. He will be all right. He grew up in the Midwest where snow is nothing. He probably thinks he can work a few hours longer."

As the snow flurries grew thicker, Pearl worried along with Nina. If anyone was to go, it should be her, not Nina. Nina had a baby to watch out for. She didn't need to be out in this kind of weather or get chilled.

"I really think I should go—"

"No." Nina held her arm. "He'll be here soon. I know it."

Beans bubbled on the back of the stove, their good smell filling the small cabin as Pearl gathered her belongings.

Tomorrow she would board the train to Portland. John would take her, not Judson Rome. She'd had all of him she could take. Of course if a heavy snow fell, they might not get to the station. The thought of staying one more night, one more day, made Pearl sad. Now that Judson Rome had forced the issue, she longed to be back with her loved ones, longed to see Paul's face again, longed to hug Mama and Emily and Ben.

Pearl thought of Emily's last letter. She said she was worried about Paul. He seemed unhappy. "Not his usual cheerful self," she said. Pearl laughed after reading that part. She felt languid a lot. Tired. Out of sorts. She wondered if her coming home would have any bearing on her feeling, or Paul's.

She smoothed her brown muslin and placed it in the trunk as the clock struck six. It was then she heard the horses outside and Nina calling out, "I thought you were never coming home."

There was silence, then John's robust laugh. "Me, an old farm boy from North Dakota would get lost in the snow? This snow is nothing by comparison."

They laughed, and Pearl came and joined in the fun. She was going to miss her friends. They truly loved one another and she would miss their company, the little house and Nina's good cooking.

At last they sat and John asked for the Lord's blessing on the food, on this the last night Pearl would be there.

"It'll all be melted by morning," John said when Pearl voiced her concern. "Snow doesn't last here like it does elsewhere."

That night Pearl hummed a song as she finished packing the trunk. Tomorrow—if the snow had melted—the children would come, pick up their papers, and she her supplies, then she'd head for the train station and soon would be on her way home—back to Portland. Would she return? Only God knew.

Pearl opened her Bible and read from James: "If any of you lack wisdom, let him ask of God, that giveth to all men liberally, and upbraideth not; and it shall be given him."

Pearl closed her Bible. Had God led her here not only to teach children, but to be a wife, a mother to three motherless children? She knew some married for conveniences' sake, but could she do that? Perhaps if Paul wasn't in her heart and mind, she might look at Judson differently. Perhaps if all hopes were dashed where

Paul was concerned—if he became betrothed to Nancy Whitfield, she might reconsider. But for now, she could think of nothing more offensive.

She closed her eyes and prayed for the snow to stop.

Old-Time Taffy

1 cup sugar
1 cup dark corn syrup
2 tablespoons water
1 tablespoon apple cider vinegar
Butter, the size of a peanut

Place ingredients in a pan; bring to a boil. Boil until it forms a hard ball in a cup of cold water. Then add 1/2 teaspoon soda; stir well.

Pour on buttered pan and when cooled, pull until shiny and ready to cut. Takes two or more to make. Try it!

This is the recipe Pearl made and took to school for the Christmas party.

seven

Just as John predicted, the snow had melted by morning. Rivers of mud ran across the dirt road in front of the house and the only indication that snow had been there was a small drift not quite melted against the north side of the barn.

It would be a short day, and Pearl knew her pay would be less than previously agreed on. John would take her to school, help her pack her things, then drive her to the train station. The children would come for that morning, pick up their belongings and say good-bye.

Nina prepared a breakfast of bacon, eggs, baking powder biscuits and her best cherry preserves. She hugged Pearl close and dabbed at her tears. "I wish things had worked out, but thee did the right thing."

"I did?"

"Yes. Everyone knows that Judson Rome is used to having his way and if he doesn't, he makes things mite uncomfortable. No godly man could act that way and you need a godly man, Pearl. There's someone there for thee. Just be patient."

Yes, there is someone for me, but is it Paul? He's not exactly a godly man. Soon she was hugging her dear friend. "We'll see each other again someday," Pearl said. "I promise."

After more tears and hugs, John placed the trunk on

the wagon.

They started out only to find Judson Rome waiting at the end of the road.

"What—?" Pearl's heart nearly stopped when she saw the fancy wagon and the pair of Morgans.

Judson hopped down and held out his hand. "I came to take Miss Galloway to school."

John said nothing, but looked at Pearl, as if he expected her to decide.

"It won't be necessary," Pearl said, trying not to spit the words out. "John will take me, then come back at noon to take me to the train station."

"That's what I wanted to talk about."

It was then Pearl noticed Mary Alice in the back of the buggy, and she was crying.

He jerked a thumb in his child's direction. "She don't want you to leave."

Pearl wanted to take the small child in her arms, tell her everything would be all right, that she'd like the next teacher just as well. "We discussed it yesterday. Everything's settled."

"But it isn't settled." Judson motioned for John to go back home. "We need to talk."

"There's nothing to say. Please stay, John," Pearl said.

"I want you to marry me," Judson said then. "No courting. Just marrying. Now. Tomorrow. Or within a week."

Pearl gripped the sides of the buggy. "But, I can't. I have said that many times over."

"Can't?" He cocked his head. "And why ever not?"

"Oh, please Miss Galloway, be my mommy," the

small voice pleaded from the backseat. "I want you to be my mommy forever and ever."

"She's been crying all morning."

For the first time, Pearl saw a tender side of Judson Rome. He was worried about his little girl, and that touched her. She tried to steady her hands in her lap. How easy it would be to say yes to the proposal. She could have her own home, a ready-made family and never have to worry about money or a roof over her head. Was this what God wanted her to do? Was this how He had answered her prayers?

Surely not. She knew Judson did not love God. Nor did he love her. He was asking her for selfish reasons. How could she marry under these circumstances?

In the end she had gone with him, just so she could console Mary Alice.

A fire was built and the Rome twins stood beaming.

"We came early so it would be warm."

"I appreciate that. Thank you."

Pearl was beginning to realize how much she would hate leaving the Stayton School. She loved all the pupils, especially the younger ones.

"Pa said you might marry him," Thomas said then. "Is that true?"

"I cannot." Pearl removed her wraps and warmed her hands by the stove. "Please do not ask why."

Judson Rome assured her the school board had someone in mind and the new teacher would arrive in January.

Soon the others came and crowded around. There were gifts of marbles, raisins, a cookie, pictures and letters. Pearl looked at each face and smiled. She might not have been here long, but she loved each one of them.

"Don't open my present until you're on the train," Mary Alice said. She held out an envelope with *Teacher* written on it.

Pearl nodded and pulled the small girl close. "And you keep learning your letters and numbers and I know you'll like the new teacher."

Cora hung back, a look of sorrow on the small, pinched face.

"Cora, what is it?"

Tears filled her eyes. "I have nothing for you, Teacher. I have no presents at my house."

"Oh, Cora, I don't need anything. Just your smile is enough to make my whole day bright."

Cora beamed, along with several others who had obviously not thought of bringing something for teacher's last day.

"Who's going to read to us now?" Thomas asked.

"Your new teacher will bring different books."

"We're sorry you're going," John Mac said then.

"And I am sorry to go, but perhaps I can come visit again one day."

All agreed that would be a good idea.

They recited the Pledge of Allegiance and Pearl read the story about the three kings bearing gifts for the Saviour, from the book of Matthew.

"We want to sing," Timothy said.

They sang several songs, and Pearl finished the morning with another reading of *The Night Before Christmas*.

It was time to go. She heard the horses outside and half expected it to be Judson Rome. But John sat on the seat, nodding when she opened the door. One more hug all around and she climbed in the wagon and looked back just once at the small log school and the waving hands. A lump came to her throat.

John helped her into the buggy. "Thee has been a good teacher. Don't forget this moment."

Pearl smiled. "Yes. I know I am a teacher, and that means more than marrying and having a family."

The trip to the train station was spent in silence as once more Pearl took in the countryside, the barren fields, long since yielding their annual harvest. A farmhouse rose on the horizon now and then, and she remembered the children she'd taught, hoping the new teacher would be a godly person and would love all of them.

At last they arrived—and none too soon as the train chugged into sight.

"Here," Pearl said, "a present for you and Nina. Just a way of thanking you both for being so loving and kind. I didn't want to give it to you sooner because Nina would have felt bad that she didn't have a going-away gift for me."

It was the cross Pearl had cross-stitched in the evening when she couldn't sleep. She could visualize it now, up over the table in the small house. "I know God will bless thee and soon a new one will join thy lives."

John looked pleased as he bent over and hugged Pearl. "Nina sent thee a lunch." John said. "Leftover chicken, biscuits and some of her special watermelon pickles."

"Thou hast been so good to me. How can I ever repay thee?"

John tipped his hat. "No need, Pearl. Thee made us plumb happy, and I truly mean it."

Soon Pearl was on the train, and found a seat at the rear of the car. *Going home, going home, going home,* the wheels clacked this time. And going home she was. Soon she'd be in the comfortable house Ben had built. Soon she'd hear the streetcars clanging down the street. Gone would be the smell of grasses blowing in the breeze, the flat land where few trees dotted the landscape. She was returning to the city, to her friends, and to the small Friends meeting she knew so well. And Paul. Somehow her heart and mind couldn't stop thinking about him. If it was meant to be, it would come to pass, but somehow she didn't think that was what God had intended for her life. She'd find out soon. He would point her in the right direction soon. Perhaps there would be more pupils to teach. At the thought of her pupils, she thought of Mary Alice's present. She'd tucked it into her valise, remembering the admonition to read it on the train.

She removed the string and laughed at the picture the child had drawn. Pearl had on her yellow dotted Swiss and stood in front of the classroom. The desk was off to the side and out of the top drawer a snake was slipping out.

Pearl laughed as she clutched the picture close. It had been a dreadful moment, but a fun one for her pupils.

She would certainly be prepared for snakes in the future, she decided, should she teach again.

The wheels clacked on: *going home, going home, going home,* lulling her to sleep.

eight

As the train pulled into the station, Pearl patted her hair into place, grabbed her bonnet and gloves, and tried to control her excitement. What if Paul had come to fetch her? What would she say? Would her expression tell how she felt?

It wasn't Paul, but a smiling, waving Ben, and she found she was just as excited. Pearl jumped down and into her brother's arms, suddenly wanting to ask about everything and everybody.

"Oh, I've never been so glad to see anyone in my whole life." She grew somber for a moment, remembering she hadn't yet told anyone that she was fired from her very first job.

"You look wonderful, little sister. That valley air must agree with you."

Pearl let her bonnet slip down her back and nodded. "I love the farming community, as you know, and the children are special, but it's good to be home!"

Ben hoisted the trunk onto the back of the wagon and started to help Pearl, then stopped. "Oh, yes, that's right. You're an independent woman now, right?"

Pearl giggled. "I suppose you might think that." She handed him the envelope Judson Rome had given her that morning. "This is for you, Ben. To help pay for me and Mama."

Ben shoved the envelope back. "I'm not taking your money. Keep it. You'll need it one day. Wait and see."

Soon they were heading for home and though she wanted to hear about Paul, she just couldn't bring herself to ask.

"And how's that little nephew of mine?"

"Growing like a weed."

"And everyone else?"

"I'm worried about Mama, if you must know." Ben's smile faded. "Still coughing. More now."

"I can't bear to think of anything happening to Mama."

"We're making her rest more these days."

"And how's work going?"

Ben smiled again. "Getting more jobs than I can handle, but I praise God for the work."

"Yes, I should think so."

"But it's Paul whom you really want to know about."

Pearl's face flushed. "I never said—"

"Sis, you didn't have to."

"Well, then. . . ." She was careful to look straight ahead. "How is he?"

"He's working across town; boarding with another fellow."

Pearl felt her hopes dashed for the second time that day. That meant she wouldn't see him tonight. Maybe she'd never see him again. Her heart suddenly stood still. He was one of the reasons she couldn't wait to get back, and now he wouldn't be there. She wanted to ask about Nancy Whitfield, but knew she'd find out soon enough. As if Ben were reading her mind, he spoke about Nancy.

"You know that woman who sits by Paul at meeting?"

"Nancy Whitfield?"

"Yes, I believe that is her name."

"I know of her."

"She isn't the sort for Paul—" Ben turned and gazed a long moment before his wide smile erupted into a half grin. "Not that you'd be caring or anything."

Pearl hit his arm. "You're teasing me."

"And why shouldn't I when it's so much fun?"

Pearl longed to say what was on her heart, her mind, but the words stayed locked inside. It would sound ludicrous to admit she cared even a tiny bit for Paul. She knew she'd never stand a chance, not when there was a beautiful woman who loved him. Why couldn't she put him out of her mind once and for all?

"So, you'll be here two weeks, then back on the train?"

"I'm not going back—"

"Not going back?"

"I don't know how to tell you this, Ben—" She braced herself, wanting to put it correctly, so all the fault did not lay with Judson Rome. "The man who hired me for the position—"

"Yes, go on." Ben was all serious now.

"He—well he didn't like my teaching methods. Said I had no control over the older boys."

"And why didn't you? I can't imagine you not cracking the whip when you can run ole Tess, the mule. You got her to move when nobody else could."

Pearl smiled at the almost forgotten memory of the mule in Iowa. "Yes, I 'spect that's true, but animals are far different from men." Her voice trailed off.

"Do go on."

"I was let go because I read one of the books Emily sent."

"One of those wild tales?

"Robinson Crusoe is not wild, but it is fiction, and I knew from the first day that Mr. Rome wanted nothing but the truth read in school."

"And you broke a rule."

Pearl took a deep breath. "I was justified."

"How?"

"The older boys wouldn't do their schoolwork, so I hit on the idea of reading once they did their numbers and English. It worked."

"What else happened that you're so carefully trying to hide from me? Remember, you can tell me when you can't go to anyone else."

"Pearl twisted her hands in her lap. "He—that is Mr. Rome—wanted to court me. He needed a mother for his children. I wasn't interested—" Her hand touched his sleeve. "Oh, Ben, he is not a kind person. I could never let myself even think of having such an uncouth man court me."

"He isn't a believer?"

"He says he believes in God, but he said such unkind remarks about the Friends."

"We have heard these things before."

"I know, but it would have been difficult for me to return, so his saying I wasn't suitable for the job was almost a blessing, except—" Sudden tears filled the pale blue eyes. "I have a dark spot on my record now."

"Nonsense!"

"It's true."

"You'll have no trouble finding a position, Pearl."

The rest of the ride was spent in gay camaraderie as Ben continued to fill Pearl in on all the happenings of Portland.

The day was gray, but at least it wasn't raining as Pearl looked around, noticing there were more buggies on the road, an occasional car and of course the street-car that clanged down Foster.

Soon the familiar and much-loved house came into sight. Pearl hopped down and ran up the walk and into the house. "Where is everyone?" she cried out.

"In the kitchen, preparing dinner," came Emily's answer as she rushed to Pearl, drying her hands on a tea towel. "Lands, but you are a sight for sore eyes."

The house was festive as Pearl knew it would be. The smell of cinnamon and sugar filled the air. "Cut-out cookies?" Pearl exclaimed, looking at the cookies lined up in a row.

She heard a chortle and turned to see baby Clifford and her mother. "Mama! I missed you so."

She hugged her mother with Clifford getting squeezed in the middle. "I never thought the holidays would come."

"Is thee remembering the reason for celebrating?"

Pearl flushed for a moment. "Perhaps, not, Mama. But God is near, He has been with me this whole time. Helping and guiding me."

"Oh, sister, I thought of thee so many times, prayed for thee, too," Emily said.

Pearl could hardly believe she was home again with those she loved and whom loved her. The picture was complete with the exception of Paul. She had so hoped to see Paul.

Pearl removed her hat and sat it on the top shelf in the entryway, straightened the wrinkles in her dress and poked some loose hair back into the knot at the nape of her neck. "It's so Christmassy—this house filled with love."

"We treasured your letters," Sarah said, easing into a chair. "I've been kind of weary with this cough hanging on—can't sleep nights. I would read and reread thy letters."

"Oh, Mama, I thought of thee and remembered what thee told me about not giving up, about praying for strength, and it worked."

Pearl thought about the happy faces, the hands waving as she left the small school that last day. Even the twins had given her a good-bye.

"I have gifts," she said aloud then. "From my students. I'll bring them out later."

"We want to hear all about it," Emily said. "Letters are fine, but don't take the place of face-to-face good ole talking."

Pearl slipped a cookie off the end of a row. The sugar melted in her mouth as she bit off the top of the star.

"We made taffy. I took it to school so we could have a party. Then Mr. Rome was angry because we were 'partying' as he put it."

"Forget Mr. Rome," Ben said. He'd been standing there and now held baby Clifford. "Thy nephew has missed thee." He held the squirming body out.

"My, but thee has grown," Pearl said. "And heavy, too."

She held the soft face next to her own and laughed when he reached for the comb in her hair.

"No, no—" It didn't keep him from reaching. "Thou must learn some manners, I see," Pearl said with a chuckle.

There was a mischievous gleam in his eye, and she knew he was going to be a stubborn, determined man someday. Probably give some teacher fits, just as Timothy and Thomas had given her.

Then she realized he smelled the cookie she'd just eaten. "Ah, that's what thee wants! A cookie. Can I, Emily? Just a tiny, teensy nibble?"

Emily nodded and handed Pearl a bell. "Just one now, mind thee. I fear he may have a sweet tooth."

And so Pearl enjoyed her second cookie, almost the whole cookie. Clifford's eyes sparkled even more as he chewed away.

"Come. It is time for this boy's bedtime." Emily reached for her son, her second born. She held him close, though he struggled to go back to his Auntie Pearl.

"Nah, nah, thee needs no more sweets!"

Pearl took the coffee Sarah handed her with the words "You must need coffee to wash down the sweets. Did thee eat lunch?"

Pearl nodded. "Nina packed me a wonderful lunch."

Pearl placed an apron over her middle and offered to finish the rolls for tomorrow's dinner. "I haven't had much chance to cook as Nina did everything. With being a working woman, my time was consumed with teaching and preparing to teach."

"Did the books come in handy that Emily sent?" Sarah asked.

"Oh, very." *I might still have the job if I hadn't read to the children,* Pearl thought, knowing there'd be time to explain it later.

The rolls were set to rise and the kitchen was quiet as Pearl slipped into a chair and took in the walls of the huge kitchen. Such a difference from the small home at the Colville's. And how she had missed the conveniences.

She thought of the running water, the indoor bathroom Ben had put in right after he and Emily married. The phone put in last year, and the electric iron. Emily hadn't thought she'd like it, but Ben said it was such a good price and they were making history by taking part on a trial basis. Pearl liked the iron and had sorely missed it when staying at the Colville's. She remembered Mama's comment, however.

"What's this world a comin' to anyhow? Too many new fangled things, if thee asks me."

"Well, Mama, times change and I guess we must go along with those changes," Ben had said, trying to reassure her. "One thing that will never change is our growing need for God and His ways." And everyone had "Amened" that.

"We'll have singing tonight around the piano," Emily

announced. "I'll take requests."

Pearl had forgotten how much she missed the piano music. It had been so much a part of her life the past two years.

She remembered then the wristlet of bells John Mac had given her. It would be the perfect gift for Clifford. He'd love the noise the bells made, the sweet sound.

Pearl waltzed around the room, throwing her arms out. "I can't believe I am here. God is so good. God has brought me home!"

≈

The evening meal, a thick beef stew, was soon on the table and Pearl was happy there were big slabs of cornbread to go with it

And for dessert, one of Emily's pies made from pie plant; one of Pearl's favorites.

"Seems you were expecting company," she said when Emily handed her a large piece of the pie.

"Of course. You are company Pearl Galloway and don't ever forget it."

Soon Pearl talked about the children, how much she liked teaching, telling about little Mary Alice who needed a mother, about the others who learned their numbers and alphabet easily. "If it weren't for the boys. They were so rowdy at first. I think Judson—Mr. Rome put his sons up to heckling me. I really do."

"Pearl's out of a job—" Ben began explaining.

And then Pearl's face crumpled up as tears spilled forth. "I tried so hard."

"There, there." Emily held her close, offering her best white linen hankie. "Tears are cleansing and thee knows that we believe that God doesn't close a door, but what he opens a window somewhere else. There's something more important for you to be doing. We just need to find out what it is."

Pearl washed dishes while Emily dried.

"I've been worried about you," Emily said.

"Worried? Because of my lack of a job?"

Emily's fingers held Pearl's wrist. "No, sister. You know you will always have a home here with us. That is why Ben built the house so large."

"What, then, is your worry?"

"Your face, Pearl. You have a worried look when you think nobody is looking. Your eyes look lost. Sad, somehow. Thee doesn't think I can tell about such things, but I can."

"If I had married Judson Rome, I would have had a nice home, children to love, but it didn't feel right. How could I love man who isn't right with God?"

"I know. I understand."

And how can I keep loving a man who doesn't know God at all? Pearl wanted to say, but she kept the thoughts locked tight inside her. *Some day it might come out, but not now. Not yet.*

"Thee has plenty of time for marriage and a family," Emily said. "Remember I was twenty-four when I met Ben."

"I remember hearing."

"I had doubts, but God directed my paths, just as he will yours."

Pearl nodded and changed the subject. "And how are Kate and Pastor Luke?"

"Fine as ever. They'll be here for dinner tomorrow night."

Pearl dried her tears. "I can hardly wait to see them."

After dishes, everyone retired to the front room where Emily sat down in front of the piano.

"I dreamed of this night so many times," Pearl said, clasping her hands in front of her. Emily playing, us singing, baby Clifford clapping his hands."

"Now, what shall I play? Any special requests?" Emily asked.

Pearl reached over and hugged Emily. "I love you, sister. So very, very much."

"And thou art loved in return more than you will ever know."

"Play 'Have Thine Own Way, Lord,'" said Pearl. "I kept humming that on the train."

"And I'll add 'Standing on the Promises,' then we'll sing Christmas carols."

Pearl sat in the front room and watched Emily's hands fly over the keys. She sang heartily, and soon Ben added his voice. Sarah could not sing; it made her cough.

"What is better than standing on the promises of God?" Ben said when the hymn was finished.

"Indeed, what more?" echoed Sarah.

"And now some carols, since the Lord's birthday is so close," Emily said.

"There is nothing more beautiful than Christmas carols. I wish we could sing them all year long."

"I suppose we could," Emily said. "Who is to say what we can and cannot sing?"

Sarah nodded. "The carols bring such deep peace to my heart. Such wonderful knowledge that our Lord reigns."

Pearl didn't add to the conversation. Instead her mind was fleeing again, thinking of a certain tall young man, remembering the first time she'd laid eyes on him in this very house, on a night much warmer than this with everyone around laughing and talking. Paul's absence left a big chunk missing from the picture. How could she make her heart content once again? Pearl knew that Paul would have been here if he cared in the same way as she did for him. "Sometimes things are not as we would wish them to be," she remembered Sarah saying. That is what she must fall back on in the days and weeks ahead.

Sarah coughed and held Clifford out toward Pearl. He was more than she could handle, especially when she started coughing. He reared up on his feet, as if wanting to fly. Pearl leaned over and gathered him in her arms. He patted her face as tears filled her eyes.

"The tree will go in the same corner as last year, Ben said. "I'll cut it down tomorrow morning."

"And we'll cover it with tinsel," Emily added. "It's the latest thing to decorate trees."

"Tomorrow we'll make more cookies and fudge and a fruitcake," Sarah pronounced.

Pearl had much to be thankful for, yet she couldn't help missing the face of a certain young man. Would he be home for Christmas? For meeting? Oh, she hoped so. Even if there wasn't a special gift for him, she knew she could make him a special treat and wrap it as a present.

"Hark the Herald Angels sing," Ben sang.

"Glory to the Newborn King." Emily joined in the singing, her fingers racing up and down the keys.

"Glory to the Newborn King!" a voice rang out, repeating the last refrain of the chorus.

"Paul!" Emily turned and smiled at her little brother. "I thought we wouldn't see you until tomorrow."

"What? And miss my best friend and sister?"

Pearl's eyes lit up, her face beaming, and without a second thought, she ran across the room and hugged him.

"It's good to have you back, Gem," he said, touching the top of her head but for a brief moment.

Pearl broke away and met his gaze. Sister, he had said. Friend. How could she expect more?

"It's wonderful to be home," she said, her gaze meeting his. "I missed all of you so much."

"Well, let's get back to the singing," Paul said. "I'm just getting wound up."

"How about 'Joy to the World'?" Emily said.

Later they sat around having second and third cups of coffee, finishing off the pie plant and sugar cookies made that morning.

"I'll make more," Emily said. "Eat away."

"Goodness, isn't it past this young man's bedtime?" Sarah asked, again holding her wriggling grandson.

"Oh, Mama, he's just wanting to be part of the festivities," Ben said. "Here. I'll take him from thee."

As if in answer, Clifford reached up and patted his father's face.

"What do you think of the nephew?" Paul asked then. "Hasn't he grown?"

"A bunch," Pearl said.

Pearl never wanted the night to end. She wanted to talk to Paul. She wanted to go out and see if the stars were out. She wanted to hear about Nancy Whitfield, see if there were any special future plans. But she said none of these things.

"I have something for you," Paul said then. "I found it in an old house we bought to fix up."

"Something for me?" Pearl repeated, wondering what it could possibly be.

"It's tattered, but you'll like it."

Tattererd? Pearl wondered what could be tattered. Paul held out a small book. With worn, brown cover, its pages musty smelling and torn, she read the title: *Black Beauty.*

"It's about a horse. Do you think you'll read it?"

"It's beautiful," Pearl answered. "Of course I'll read it. And Emily will, too. I'll treasure it always and forever." She glanced up, thinking he was taller than she remembered. Taller than she was.

He laughed. "That's my Pearl. Always happy. Always smiling."

Ben scooted his chair back. "It's time for bed. We've got a full day ahead of us."

Paul grasped Pearl's hand for a moment. "I'm glad to see you looking so well."

Pearl felt her face flush as she finally looked away. "You're even taller than I remember," she murmured.

Everyone left the room, but Pearl stood in the doorway, watching as Paul moved toward the back door and thinking of how his eyes had met hers.

He hesitated, then turned around. "It's good that you're home." His gaze lingered, and Pearl felt her face flush.

Finally she climbed the stairs to the bedroom she shared with her mother. *My Pearl,* he'd said. Of course that didn't mean anything, but she liked the way it sounded, the way he had looked at her, the special book he'd kept for her.

If it were summer, she might have sat on the porch for a while and counted the stars with Paul. If tomorrow weren't Christmas Eve, she might have stayed up and read *Black Beauty.* But she could not do either. It had been a full day, and she needed her rest.

nine

Sarah was coughing into her pillow when Pearl entered the bedroom.

"Mama." Pearl leaned over and rubbed her mother's back. "Thy cough seems worse."

"I'll be okay." She reached out and took Pearl's hand and held it against her cheek. "It's good to have you back home, daughter. I been a-laying here a-thinkin' about you and how beautiful you've become."

Pearl felt color rise to her cheeks. "Mama, you know I have never been beautiful, not one single day of my life."

"No, child, you have a radiance that catches the eye."

I wish it would catch a certain gentleman's eye, Pearl wanted to say, but of course she didn't.

"We missed thee terrible while thee was gone," Sarah went on.

"And I missed you and all the others," Pearl said, going over and putting an arm around her mother's broad shoulders.

"Thou must go after what thee needs," Sarah said, as she crawled under a comforter.

"Mama, whatever do you mean?"

Pearl fussed with the sheet, tucking it in. Her mother had always been wise. Perceptive. Had she meant what Pearl thought she did? Could she possibly know how she felt about Paul?

"God can't answer a prayer if thy request isn't made." Sarah squeezed Pearl's hand again. "It's time to start asking, my child. 'Ask and it shall be given you; seek and ye shall find.'"

Pearl eased out of her best dress and hung it over a chair.

"There is one prayer I used to say many times over—"

"What was that, Mama?"

"That I might see my children again before I die."

Pearl thought of the others. Mama had Ben and her. Jesse had come and gone, but she knew Mama missed Anna who had stayed behind in Iowa to be a nurse. Clara lived in far-off Connecticut. And Lulu was in California.

"I wonder if Albert is in Washington still—on the coast I believe Ben said?"

Sarah nodded. "He doesn't write. The girls do write sometimes. They are busy. Happy. I should be happy, too."

&

Pearl wondered now, as she often had wondered why she was so tall and manly looking. Mama was tall, but not as tall as Pearl. Anna was tall, as were Clara and Lulu, but Pearl was the tallest and had the broadest shoulders. In spite of Sarah's words, Pearl felt big and bulky and downright ugly. She dismissed the idea from her mind immediately. No sense in dwelling on it, she reminded herself.

"Mama, do you want me to read from the Bible?"

Sarah nodded. "I love to hear thy voice, Pearl. It has such a wonderful quality to it. Lilting. Expectant."

The worn Bible automatically opened to Proverbs, and Pearl found one of her favorite passages.

> *Trust in the Lord with all thine heart;*
> *and lean not unto thine own understand-*
> *ing.*
> *In all thy ways acknowledge him,*
> *and he shall direct thy paths.*
> *Be not wise in thine own eyes:*
> *fear the Lord, and depart from evil.*

"He knows what is good for me, for us," Pearl said. Sarah's eyes were closed, but she wasn't asleep yet. "When I think of how many times you have read Scripture to me—"

Sarah's ragged breathing filled the room. Pearl knotted her hands. She wouldn't think about it. Mama was invincible. She would always be there.

Pearl turned off the lamp and sat in the darkness, listening to Mama breathe. She wanted to talk more, wanted to ask what was meant about "going after what thee needs." Did Sarah know about the young and beautiful Nancy Whitfield? Did Sarah really know what was inside Pearl's heart, how she felt? Mama was wise. Mama knew things just by looking and listening. Yes, Mama must know or she wouldn't have said what she did. Was there a chance that Paul might someday love her? Was there a chance that he might find God and make him real in his life?

Pearl thought of Judson Rome. He wanted a marriage of convenience, and even if he didn't love her, she could have accepted that. But not loving God with all his heart and soul bothered her more. She was glad to be gone, though she'd always worry about the children. What was to become of Mary Alice? Thomas and Timothy? And John Mac? Cora and the others? Would the new teacher love them?

Clifford's hearty cry interrupted Pearl's thoughts. Strange for him to be getting up at this time of night. He was sleeping straight through now, Emily said. Pearl reached for a robe and slipped it around her shoulders before tiptoeing down the steps to the nursery.

Emily had not come. Had she not heard him? Pearl opened the nursery door and there he was standing up in his cradle.

"Goodness, gracious, if you're not careful, you're going to fall right out on your head." She leaned over and picked him up.

He laughed and patted her face.

"You missed me, didn't you?" She held him tight against her cheek. "I know I missed you. Yes, even your crying."

She changed his diaper and gown and wrapped him in the blanket. Maybe if she rocked him for a while, he'd go back to sleep. There was a rattling in his chest, but it was cold season. The winter winds had whipped up from the east and seemed to engulf the house. Pearl started humming a tune she especially liked.

" 'Have thy own way, Lord, have thine own way.' "

"I expect if anyone gets his own way around here, it's young Clifford." Ben stepped into the room. "I wondered why he shut up so quickly."

"He just wanted his auntie to rock him."

"Can I get you anything?" Ben asked.

"Brother, do you remember anything at all about Grandpa and Grandma Galloway? Or Mama's parents?"

"Sprouse," Ben said then. "Her maiden name was Sprouse. And no, I don't know anything about either of them." He set across from Pearl. "Why does thee ask?"

"Just wondering why I am so tall." She wanted to say "and ugly," but knew Ben would admonish her just as Sarah did. They both thought she was pretty, but that was because they were family and loved her.

"Saw a photo once," Ben said then. "Ma probably has it somewhere in her treasure box."

"Of her parents?"

"Yes," Ben said. "Seems her father was tall and her mother, too. It's an asset to be tall," Ben said then, as if reading Pearl's mind. "Lots of people wish they were tall."

Clifford started jabbering as if he wanted to add his opinion to the discussion. Ben got up, leaned over and took the smiling baby from Pearl. "And, you, young man need to get back to bed. It is not morning."

"Emily didn't hear him?"

Ben frowned. "She did, but I told her to rest. She's having some problems again—I hope she'll be okay."

"Problems?" Pearl asked.

"I don't think she's fully recovered from Clifford's birth." Ben held his small son close. "I just thank God every day for such a healthy, robust child."

"I'll get up with him at night," Pearl offered.

Ben touched her shoulder. "Thanks, Pearl. You're such a help and blessing to us all. We'll manage just fine now that you're back home again."

Soon Clifford was back in bed, with Ben commanding him to be quiet in the authoritative voice fathers often have.

"I'll wait until he's asleep," Pearl said.

"Sometimes when he stays fussy, I put him in the buggy and rock him over a log."

"Over a log?"

"Yes. Seems he likes the bumpy part. Calms him down and makes him sleep."

"Well, I can try it," Pearl said, but he had already closed his eyes and was sound asleep. Pearl crept back up the stairs, thankful once again to be home where she belonged.

❧

The night was chilly, but Paul didn't seem to notice as he made his way to his room at one end of the shed. He had a lantern to see by. Not that he needed to see. His heart pounded and he wondered if he'd be able to sleep at all this night. This Christmas Adam.

He chuckled when he thought about Christmas Adam. It was something he and Pearl talked about last year.

"If December twenty-fourth is Christmas Eve, then the twenty-third should be Christmas Adam," she had said, laughing. "Didn't Adam come before Eve?"

Paul had agreed that her reasoning was sound. "So? What do we do? How do we celebrate?"

"We must prepare our hearts for the Lord's birth."

Paul remembered how he had changed the subject. He didn't want to talk about God—not then. Not now. He just couldn't believe as they all did. He was still seeking answers, searching for truths.

Searching. Seeking. He lay on his bed and stared at the rough walls of the shed. One thing he knew was how he felt about Pearl. He'd admonished himself many times in the two months she'd been gone, saying he didn't care for her in that way. She was his sister-in-law. They enjoyed each other's company. That had to be enough. Yet there was something in her eyes. The way she met his gaze and didn't look away. He had seen it before. He had wondered about it. Could she possibly care for him?

Nancy Whitfield had that look when she talked to him, but try as he might, he felt nothing but friendship while in her presence. His heart didn't beat faster, nor did his palms feel sweaty as they had tonight.

Pearl's voice. Her laugh. The way she walked. And held baby Clifford. He wanted to see her holding their child in that same loving way.

He rolled over and pounded the floor. Pearl didn't seem to be the marrying type. He had to forget her and concentrate on his work.

He lit the lamp and pulled a box out from under the bed. Inside lay the design for the house he wanted to build. He picked up the tablet and sketched the scene from tonight. Clifford with his hands flying, the bells jingling. . . . Ben standing beside Emily at the piano, his voice filling the room. . . . Sarah, her gray head held high as she listened and watched and tried to stifle her coughing. . . . Emily's fingers running up and down the keyboard of the magnificent piano that only she could play. . . . Then Pearl. His beloved Pearl. Talking. . . laughing. . . singing. . . . Her gaze as it rested on his face. The hair, thick and brown with a silver comb in the side. . . .

Paul set the sketch aside and wrote some words on the next page. It was a poem of sorts. It was one way he could get his thoughts down. He'd mentioned it to Emily shortly after she'd given him the sketchbook.

"Men don't write poems, sis."

Her hand rested on his shoulder. "Oh, yes, they do, Paul. They write poems and books and stories and they are all so beautiful."

Could he be a plasterer and an artist? A poet? Was that what God would have him do?

He pushed the box under the bed and lay on his back, wondering how God had crept into his thoughts like that. He had underlined a verse in the Bible, "He will direct thy paths" and wondered if God could be directing him. If God cared, as Emily and the others claimed, He would have the answers. Paul just had to figure out what they were. And he guessed one of the ways would be through talking. Prayer. That's what they called prayer.

Paul thought of the long moments of silent prayer at Meeting Day. He always found his mind wandering off on the next day's job, or later on he'd think of Pearl at the other end of the aisle. And Nancy would come sit beside him, as if she belonged there. He didn't want her there. He couldn't think of her in the way she thought of him. One couldn't court one lady if his thoughts were on another, could he?

"God," Paul said aloud. "Show me how to pray. I want to talk to You about a few things." Then he smiled. "Actually, I think I already have. Amen."

"Happy Christmas Adam," he said, rolling over and giving his pillow a hard jab.

ten

Breakfast was a flurry of cooking, baking and making pots of coffee. Ben and Paul had gone after the tree. Ben had seen one of the right size on a lot he owned, and they would be back with the Douglas fir in a few minutes.

Pearl clasped her hands in delight when she saw and smelled the huge tree. Clifford clapped.

"You're such a mimic," Emily said, looking at her small son and remembering how lonely last year had been with no baby to share their job.

"He should put the first decoration on the tree," Pearl said. "And I have just the thing."

She went to her trunk and brought out the chains and snowflakes. The colorful paper chains could be draped around the tree while the snowflakes could be pinned onto the branches.

"These are gifts from my class."

"I just bet those students will be happy to have you back," Paul said. Pearl grimaced. Paul didn't know. He hadn't been here when they had discussed it and the two of them hadn't had a chance to talk.

"She isn't going back," Ben said.

"But why ever not?"

"I was not suitable, according to Judson Rome, head of the Marion School Board."

"He brought Pearl there under false pretenses," Ben added.

Pearl couldn't quite look at Paul. What must he be thinking about her? That she couldn't finish a task she'd started?

"He wanted a wife, a mother for his children," Ben continued. "Pearl could not concede to marry a man who does not serve God."

Now it was Paul's turn to grimace. Of course Pearl would only marry a godly man, should she choose to marry one day. That definitely meant he did not have a chance. What had made him think there was a certain look in her eyes?

Since he was the tallest, Paul put a golden star at the top. This time Clifford clapped his hands first.

"The star of Bethlehem," Sarah said. "It's there to guide us, just as it guided the shepherds of long ago."

Pearl wrapped her chains around the tree and added a few snowflakes. The strings of popcorn and cranberries were Sarah's contribution, since it was something she could do while sitting.

Emily brought out the tinsel. "This is supposed to look like rain."

"Rain!" Ben sputtered. "We get enough rain here. We don't need to make the false stuff to help us remember."

Everyone laughed and agreed. Still Emily wanted the shiny tinsel to adorn the tree, the baby's very first tree. She had to hold Clifford, as he wanted to crawl over and get into the tree.

"I can just see him pulling the whole tree down," Ben said.

"Yes, thee is right," Emily said. "He must be watched very closely."

"It's a gorgeous tree," Pearl said after the tinsel was added. "The most beautiful one I've ever seen."

Paul stood close, wanting to say something, but he couldn't even answer an affirmative. It was beautiful, but not as beautiful as the woman who had just decorated it.

"We have to work!" Ben said then. "Thou knowest what it says in Proverbs chapter six, verse six: 'Go to the ant, thou sluggard; consider her ways, and be wise.'"

"'And an idle soul shall suffer hunger,'" Emily added, quoting the second part of Proverbs 19:15.

Ben grinned. "C'mon, Paul, help me finish the roof on the lean-to."

"And we will finish our baking," said Emily heading to the kitchen.

Sarah sat at the table, peeling apples, while Pearl rolled out enough dough for three apple pies. She knew apple was Paul's favorite. She might even make him an extra tart if there were scraps left.

"I can hardly wait to see Luke and Kate," Pearl said, breaking the silence.

"Thee hasn't seen them since thee went away to teach school."

"I'll change into my best dress, the one Kate made, before they arrive."

Paul didn't come in for the noon meal and Pearl wondered what he was doing in the shed. She heard pounding and knew it must be a Christmas gift.

The food was prepared, gifts wrapped and under the

tree, and a roast chicken and ham filled the kitchen with delicious smells. The Galloways adhered to the rule of no working on Sunday, and tomorrow—Christmas—was on Sunday this year. There would be plenty of leftovers for the morrow. Ben had bought oranges at the farmer's market downtown, and they sat in a bowl on top of the piano, next to the blue candles Emily had placed there yesterday.

The table was set with Emily's bright red tablecloth. Everyone had washed up and dressed in their finest. Pearl wore the sprigged calico and brushed her hair out, then braided it one long braid which she left cascading down her back. It was her dress-up hairdo.

She helped Sarah into a dark percale she saved for Sunday meeting day, and together they went downstairs. "I love thee, Mama."

"And I, thee, child."

"I've been thinking about what thou said last night. I think Ben should try to reach everyone. Maybe we can have a big family reunion."

"It's too far for all to come." Sarah coughed into her handkerchief.

Pearl tried to steady herself as she helped Sarah down the final step. "I'll see what Ben thinks." *And he'd better not wait if they are to arrive in time*, she thought.

Kate and Luke arrived at five sharp. Pearl heard the horses draw up out front and opened the door and ran out without waiting to put a wrap on.

"Kate! Luke!" she cried, hugging first one, then the other. "Merry Christmas!"

"And Merry Christmas to thee, too," Kate said. "It's wonderful to see thee again!"

Luke nodded. "Thou art just as pretty as ever, I see. And excitable, too."

Pearl felt her cheeks flush. "Excitable is right, but the pretty is not."

"Have ye not heard 'Beauty is in the eye of the beholder'?" Luke asked. His eyes twinkled. Or as a man once said, " 'give me beauty in the inward soul.' I believe his name was Plato."

"Oh, thou and thy history lesson," Kate said, hugging her husband.

"Come in, come in!" Ben stood in the doorway, beckoning the Morrisons in.

Kate wore a full-skirted scarlet dress with lace at the collar and cuffs. Tiny jewel buttons decorated the bodice.

Her cheeks were pink from the long ride, and she discarded her heavy cloak and wide-brimmed hat. Combs decorated the dark hair. She would always be beautiful, Pearl thought as she felt a sudden tightness in her chest.

"I see thee is lovely as always," Ben said, kissing Kate's cheek.

"And an early Merry Christmas to the Galloways!" Luke said, coming in and hugging Sarah.

Clifford, up from his nap, jumped up and down in a chair Ben had made for him. It kept him out of trouble, yet he could bounce.

"I thought we would never arrive," Kate said, "but we had fun singing songs and reciting Bible verses from memory. The sky is full of stars!"

Luke looked at his wife adoringly. "Kate makes an adventure out of everything, and that is why God loves her so."

"And us, too," said Ben.

Soon the eight sat around the huge oak table and filled their plates with Emily's good cooking. Then Luke asked the blessing:

"God, our father, we thank Thee for this special occasion—that of Thy Son's birth. We thank Thee for friends. For warm, comfortable homes. For family. For blessings not yet received, and for this food prepared for us as we celebrate and remember Thee."

"Hear ye! Let's eat!" declared Ben.

Pearl could hardly swallow. So much had happened in the day since she'd come home. She stared at the gravy, then glanced up. Paul was watching her. She waved her fork at him and smiled.

"We are wanting to hear all about thy teaching job and thy pupils," Luke said.

"I shall tell thee all about it later," Pearl said. "Over pie and coffee."

"After we open the gifts," Emily added.

New mittens came from Emily, while Sarah's gift was stocking caps for all. Pearl was glad she'd knitted stockings. Ben's gift was books for the three younger women: Emily, Pearl and Kate.

"If I was handy with knitting needles, I would have made my gifts," Ben said. "Not enough time for whittling gifts these days."

"I love books," Pearl said, holding hers close.

Emily looked at her book of poems and read the

inscription from Ben. "To My Emily, the light of my life."

Pearl's *Uncle Tom's Cabin* was inscribed to: "Pearl, the best sister in the world."

Kate's book was poetry, and Sarah had a new Bible, all leather covered and soft, just the right size for her arthritic hands to hold.

Baby Clifford had a jaunty new little cap in brown corduroy. "I couldn't resist," said Ben.

Pearl watched while everyone opened their stockings.

"Thy knitting is much tighter, I see," said Sarah, holding a sock up.

"I'm glad thee likes it." She saw Paul leave the room and wondered where he was going. He had not opened the gift from her, though she knew he could tell it was a pair of socks. She wished now she'd thought of something different. A surprise.

Clifford was enjoying the noise the paper made when he tore it. Everyone watched him and didn't notice Paul until he came into the room holding a framed picture out for all to see.

"My gift for this family," he said.

All crowded around to see the fine pencil sketch—a gathering around the piano as everyone sang carols.

"Oh, Paul, it is lovely!" Emily looked as if she was about to cry. All agreed.

"And the frame?" Ben asked.

"That's what I was making today."

Pearl said nothing as she stared at the picture, looking at each one's face. But it was her face she looked at the longest. Paul had made her beautiful. Her eyes. Her face. This didn't look like her, did it?

"I have another smaller one for you, Gem," he said, holding out a small sketch.

Pearl looked at it, then held it out for all to see. "Paul—it's wonderful. I adore it."

And, again, she noticed that she looked almost pretty.

"I'd say thee captured our Pearl's face quite well," Luke said then.

"And I say we need to sing songs!" Pearl said, not wanting her loved ones to keep staring at her.

"There's another gift," Paul said, "a poem I wrote to you. It was a long time ago, but I was afraid to give it to you before."

"Thou hast given me enough, but I'd be honored to own one of thy poems along with the drawing."

"I do miss thy playing, Emily," Luke said. "We have found no one yet to play the piano in our small gathering of souls."

It was because of the new church that Luke and Kate would stay but one night. They would rise early to return home to have the first Christmas service at noon in their small, crude church.

Kate stood and raised her arm. She liked secrets and had waited to share the good news.

"We will be parents come summer," she announced, grabbing Luke's arm before sitting down.

"I knew it," Sarah said. "Thee had a glow, as mothers-to-be often have. A sweater I've been knitting is already too small for our robust Clifford."

"Sarah, how wonderful."

"Seems we have much to be thankful for as the old year draws to a close," Ben said. "We'll pray for a healthy child."

"I'll say Amen, brother," Luke said.

Pearl knew Luke's heart must still ache for the small child lost, along with his first wife, a few years ago in Ohio. His son was in heaven with Isobelle, Ben and Emily's newborn who had died.

Surely God would bless this child of Kate and Luke's.

Later after wrappings were cleared up, Luke and Kate packed the buggy for their return trip.

"You take care," everyone shouted as the Morrisons left. Amid waving hands and choruses of "good-bye until next trip," they started off.

"And Merry Christmas!" Pearl added.

Soon they were back inside and bedding down for the night. Pearl found her presents under the tree, where she'd placed them. The sketch from Paul was so beautiful. She touched the lines, the eyes, with the crinkles at the end. It was something she would treasure always.

"Do you really like it?" Paul stood behind her.

Pearl's face beamed. "It's my best gift," she said, her gaze meeting his. "I never knew you were an artist."

"I'm not."

"Oh, yes, you are, Paul. This picture and the other one is wonderful. You captured each one's expression so well. Except," she paused.

"Except?"

"I think—" But she couldn't say it.

"You think yours is not a good likeness—"

"I never said that."

"But you think it, Gem. I can tell."

"Thou made me pretty," she said finally.

"Because you are," Paul said. "Everyone thinks it, but you."

Pearl looked away. Could it be true? Did she look pretty to others?

"I thank you for thy gift and for the compliment. Merry Christmas, Paul."

"Merry Christmas, Pearl."

He turned and walked out of the house while Pearl sat in the darkness, cherishing this moment. If she lived to be a hundred, she would never forget this Christmas Eve, this wonderful, precious day.

eleven

As it turned 1911 William Howard Taft was still president. Not that it mattered to the family on Foster Road. The new year brought little change to the Galloway household.

Ben worked hard building houses, rain or not. Paul's work was mostly indoors, and he kept busy. Emily was sick mornings, and Pearl knew she must be in the family way again. She seemed more tired now. Sarah's cough was worse, and the doctor said if she could go where the sun came out every day, if she could find warmth, she would get better, but Sarah wanted to stay in Portland with her family.

Pearl did not seek another teaching position. She was needed at home. Clifford was too much for Mama to handle, and Emily was sick each morning. It was up to Pearl to cook, to put the house in order. Ben insisted she not try to find work. At least not yet.

Letters about Sarah's condition had been written to all but Jesse. So far nobody had answered except Clara: "I want to come visit you, Mama, but the doctor says I cannot travel. You will have another grandchild in a few months. I love you. God bless."

Sarah slept much of the day, though she was often restless.

Pearl now slept downstairs, where she could be close

to Clifford. Her heart and mind thought of what might be, but for now she was too busy working and praying for more sun so Mama could go out and sit in the sunshine.

January turned to February, then March came. It seemed as if many months had passed since she had taught at the Stayton School. She knew school would be out soon so the older ones could help plant crops. She wondered about Mary Alice, Cora, John Mac and the twins. Any day now they might hear that Nina had delivered her baby.

It was on Saturday that Luke suddenly showed up at the Galloway's.

"Kate, is she all right?" Pearl asked. She'd stopped ironing a dress when the knock sounded.

"Kate is fine."

"What is it then?" Pearl knew by the look on his face that something had happened.

"I just received word that Harrison Drake has had a stroke. And Beulah—bless her heart—is not doing well, either. She has the cough—similar to Sarah's. It may be tuberculosis, though she has not seen a doctor recently."

"A stroke! Oh, no. I must tell Emily."

"I will do that, Pearl."

Luke set his hat on the table in the foyer, and Pearl followed him to the bedroom where Emily was resting. She looked up from her diary.

"Luke!"

"Emily, I had to come tell thee, as I did not know what to do."

"What is it? Ben?"

"It's your grandparents. Both are gravely ill, and though Harrison was taking care of Beulah, he's had a stroke and is bedridden. A neighbor had been coming in once a day, but she can no longer do this. Does thee know of anyone who could go? See that they are taken care of?"

"Anna," Pearl said. "My sister Anna is a nurse, but she's in Iowa."

"I should go." Emily stood, then held onto the bedpost to keep from falling.

"No!" Pearl cried, reaching out to steady her. "You are not strong enough."

"The sickness is better. Someone must help, and it should be me."

"No." Pearl almost shouted. "If it's anyone, it will be me."

"Pearl, you can't mean this. You're not a nurse, and why should this be your burden?"

"Because we're family, and families help each other. I'm the strongest and most suited to go."

Emily nodded, not even sure her grandparents would accept her help. They had yet to forgive her for marrying Ben, a non-Quaker, and for being ungrateful and deserting them.

"It is true," Luke said in agreement. "Pearl should go. At least for now. Save your strength, Emily."

"I know it's right for me," Pearl said suddenly with complete conviction. "I am not teaching now and just get in the way around here. I thought about applying at the candy factory where Kate and Emily used to work, but if I'm needed there, that is what I should do."

In the end Emily agreed. She pulled Pearl close. She loved Pearl more than she could have ever loved a sister. How could she do this so readily, so easily?

"I don't know a lot about nursing, but I should certainly be able to build a fire, cook the meals and bring in water and medicine for the patient."

"You'll do a fine job," Luke said. "And God will bless thee for doing this far more than you can imagine. God has a wonderful life ahead for you. You are a true server if ever I saw one."

Pearl knew she would miss seeing Paul every night when he got off work—miss his smile, their conversations. But she was needed elsewhere, and it was something she felt led to do.

She packed a bag and left with Luke that afternoon.

"It will seem primitive," Luke warned, helping her into the buggy.

"No worse than our house in Iowa," she said, her chin jutting out.

"Art thou doing this for another reason, one you want to talk about?"

She stood, staring at Luke, wondering why he would ask such a question.

"Very well, Luke. I will talk to thee, though I could tell no other. Not even Emily."

"Your words are safe with me, my friend."

"It is Paul."

"Paul?"

Pearl knotted the linen handkerchief. "I find myself being drawn to him, and can't get him out of my heart.

I know it is not good. Paul doesn't serve God, and—"

"Pearl, you cannot sit in judgment for any of God's children."

"But we have talked many times. He says he cannot believe. I fear he may end up like Jesse."

Luke looked pensive. "Some of this might be true, but I think he believes more than he realizes." Luke had seen a noticeable change in the young man, and was confident it was only a matter of time before he, too, would seek God as his Saviour. But could he say this to Pearl? What if Paul didn't feel as she did? It could do far more harm if he were to give her hope and it turned out to be false. No, he could not tell her this, yet he thought of the Christmas drawing, remembering the look Paul had captured.

He had made Pearl beautiful, made his love come through.

"Remember where it says that God cares for thee, that God will always take care of thee?"

Pearl nodded. "I believe that."

"I think the time is coming when you will have your answer, my child. But I need to say something about Paul. Never, ever would he be like Jesse. I know him well enough to know what is in his heart, and he is not the type of man to consort to several women. When Paul finds the woman he loves, he will be true to her to the end."

Pearl felt her cheeks redden and she didn't know why. Paul had never indicated his feelings, yet a tiny shred of hope spread through her. She stared back at Luke's kind, thoughtful face, thankful she could talk to him.

"Kate did not believe for a long while. I loved her in silence, Pearl. I, like you, knew it was wrong, but God in His infinite glory made the change in Kate. Without killing her beautiful spirit, she came to believe God's plan for her life. No man could ask for more."

Pearl sat and pondered what Luke said. She knew Kate had given up dancing and didn't mind it. Perhaps he was right. Maybe Paul would come to believe one day, too. She had to believe it.

ɞ

The horses had stopped and Pearl got her first glimpse of the Drake homestead. The old house was in need of a fresh coat of paint. Pearl wondered if it had ever seen paint.

"Let me tell thee about the Drakes," Luke began. "Before you go in, you must understand that Beulah has a strong mind, a determined one. Bless her heart, she has never known how to be kind."

"I know this from things Emily has said. I believe I can handle that." She thought about Judson Rome. His overbearing ways had cost her the teaching job. Beulah Drake couldn't be worse.

"Pearl, it is wonderful for thee to do this. I have no way of knowing how long it will be before Beulah is back on her feet—or Mr. Drake."

Pearl squared her shoulders. "Well, I think we'd better go inside and see just exactly what my duties will be."

Luke nodded and the two walked up the overgrown path. He hesitated just a moment before lifting his hand and knocking on the heavy wooden door.

"Just say a prayer that I will meet Mrs. Drake's standards."

"That I will," Luke said. "That we all will."

The door opened and a woman stood there, crying.

"Are you the person coming to help?"

Pearl stepped forward. "I am."

"Well, bless you, honey. I hope you have more fortitude than I do."

And without another word, she grabbed her coat and hurried up the path.

"Yes," Luke said, touching Pearl's arm. "Thee will need all the prayers we can muster. And I must go in first to see Sister Beulah."

Pearl followed Luke down the hall, noticing its cobwebs and unkempt appearance. The house looked as if it could stand a good spring cleaning, and she figured she had come none too soon.

twelve

Pearl's days became a blur as she cared for the Drakes. Mr. Drake was no problem, though she had to feed him and most of the food dribbled down his chin into his neck.

Mrs. Drake, however, had a sharp tongue and Pearl soon realized it was best to ignore her. She was sick and people were not at their best when sick. Not that Beulah had ever been at her best.

But it was the grueling housework that wore her to a frazzle. Though not used to carrying water, she carried several buckets those first few days because everything had to be washed and cleaned.

She washed all the dishes in the cupboards and the curtains and the floors. She pounded the front-room rug and shook the small rugs until she could shake no more.

Soon the kitchen sparkled with clean cabinets, floors and walls. Then everything was dusted and even the parlor was cleaned thoroughly.

"What is thee doing?" Beulah asked each day when Pearl wasn't sitting beside her. Pearl felt she must make excuses because she could hardly say, "I was cleaning your dirty house."

Pearl read a lot at the Drake's. She read the Bible aloud to Mr. Drake, but he didn't seem to know if she was there or not. When the doctor came, he explained to Pearl that Mr. Drake knew more than he let on. That he could hear and assimilate; he just couldn't answer. He also said it was good to continue reading and talking to him—that it might help him to get well sooner.

So Pearl had continued. When she fed him the clear broth and most of it dribbled out and down onto his napkin, she smiled and patted his hand. "It's okay, Mr. Drake. Some of it's getting inside you." She had to laugh, as it was like trying to feed baby Clifford. He would spit out more than he kept inside his tiny mouth. Mr. Drake certainly didn't spit, but he had no control over his lips.

Pearl felt sorry for him. She remembered Emily saying how kind and wonderful he had always been. Now the eyes stared blankly ahead. She wished she knew what else to do for him, but since there was nothing, she kept him as warm and comfortable as possible.

Mrs. Drake, as Pearl thought of her, since she could never call her by her first name, was another matter. She seemed to like being critical, cross and crotchety. She wondered if she had been this bad when Emily lived here and somehow thought she probably had. She wanted so much to be up and about, taking care of her house and especially the kitchen. She complained when Pearl brought cool soup. She didn't like strong coffee, weak tea, and the baking powder biscuits were far from flaky. The only thing Pearl had ever made that she liked was apple pie.

Pearl had to smile when she thought about apple pie. Paul always liked her pie. Once when she had made pie plant pie, he had eaten it, but didn't ask for seconds. When she asked why not, he smiled. "Because I prefer your apple pie."

It was good that Pearl knew what to make to make him happy. She could hardly wait to go back home and to work in the sunny, yellow kitchen. The kitchen here, in spite of her cleaning it, was dark and dreary.

Pearl sighed. Of course she had no idea when she could go home again. Mrs. Drake could go on forever with this coughing condition, and stroke victims, though bedridden, often lived a long time, according to the doctor. It was not a bright prospect. Still, she was glad she could do it.

The little bell tinkled then and Pearl rushed to see what Mrs. Drake wanted.

"My photo album," the older woman said. "It's in the parlor. I must have it immediately."

"Of course." Pearl didn't know where in the parlor, but knew she could find it.

It was heavy and very old. It smelled musty too as she lifted it and carried it to the bedroom.

"I want to show you what my parents looked like. I also wanted to know if you would give this to Emily and Paul."

"Emily and Paul?" It was the first Pearl realized that Mrs. Drake knew who she was.

"Come now. Don't think I'm a simpleton. Of course you belong to Benjamin. One look at your face and the broad shoulders and I knew who you were, where you came from."

Pearl sputtered. "Why did you let me stay then since

you dislike my brother so?"

Mrs. Drake's eyes widened as she was about to snap back, but it was as if she thought better of it and closed her mouth. She opened the album and pointed to a couple sitting on a small settee.

"I do not dislike Benjamin. He just isn't right for Emily."

"He loves Emily," Pearl countered. She did not want to hear cross words where her beloved brother was concerned.

"That may very well be, but he was not raised a Quaker."

"He loves the church and the people and worships and loves God," Pearl said, again coming to her brother's defense.

"Humph! There's no point in discussing this further."

Pearl longed to discuss it. She longed to tell Mrs. Drake how wrong she had been, how wrong she was now not to want to see Emily again, not to want to see the baby Clifford. How could she treat Emily with such disdain?

"Would you like a cup of tea? It's nigh on to four."

"After I finish showing you this."

Mrs. Drake identified several photos, then closed the heavy book. "These are photos that belong to Emily and Paul. They are of their paternal side. I want them to be taken and valued."

Pearl held the book close. "I know Emily will like having them, Mrs. Drake."

"Very well. Don't get maudlin on me. Go fetch the tea. And you'd better check on Mr. Drake. I have a feeling about him."

Pearl went to the other bedroom first. He had moved. She knew it. He was still lying on his back, his gaze fixed on the ceiling, but he was looking toward the window, toward the winter sunshine streaming in through the window. She was sure he had moved, even if only a few inches.

"And it's the sunshine you're a-wanting to see?" Pearl asked. She pulled the curtains back just a bit so he could see into the yard. Perhaps this meant he was going to be all right after all. She leaned over and straightened his pillow just a bit, then folded the top sheet down over the layer of quilts. His sudden grunting sound made her jump.

"Mr. Drake, you're trying to tell me something. Oh, what is it? If only I knew what it was."

Pearl thought about opening the window, but knew it was too cold. Still, a bit of fresh air might be invigorating for him.

She went over and pulled up until just a small bit of air filled the room. She looked back. "There now! Is that what you wanted?"

His expression did not change, nor did he move or make any more noise.

Pearl looked out the window. An evergreen tree filled the corner and a smell of pine hit her nose. Spring was definitely in the air.

"I am going to make some tea. I'll be back with a cup after I take Mrs. Drake hers."

There. Again, she thought she detected a small bit of movement.

Pearl hummed as she poured the water that was still hot on the back of the big old-fashioned cook stove. A bit of sugar for Mrs. Drake, but plain for Mr. Drake. Doctor's orders.

"Is he all right? My husband?" Beulah asked when Pearl came in with the tray and two cups. "I heard you talking to him."

"He moved."

"Moved?"

"Yes. He turned toward the window so I opened the curtain a bit more."

But that's impossible."

"He did. I'm sure of it."

"We'll tell the doctor when he comes."

Beulah stirred her tea and watched as Pearl left with the other cup.

She helped lift Mr. Drake's head, raising the cup to his lips. Did she only imagine it, or had he actually swallowed more than usual? "There now, you're not as messy today." She smiled, bent down and kissed his lined forehead. It was cool, almost clammy, as always. Pearl thought of Emily and what she might do if she came to visit. What if she came to see her grandfather, but stayed out of Beulah's room?

"Mr. Drake, I know Emily wants to come to see you. She wants to express her concern for you—play some of the hymns you love, sit and talk to you. I wonder— would it be okay if I were to bring her with me next week?"

Pearl looked, but the face seemed expressionless. If only he could communicate. There had to be a way.

She couldn't help but think that Emily's presence would make him feel better. Might make him want to try to talk again. It was worth a try in spite of how Mrs. Drake felt.

Pearl left the room, but closed the window and drew the curtains. The sunshine had left and soon it would be dark out. Tonight they would have leftover soup from yesterday. And sugar cookies for dessert.

She hummed as she stirred up biscuit dough and put the pot of potato soup on the stove. Thoughts of Paul flashed across her mind again. How she missed seeing him. How she wanted to go back to how things had been before. Evenings spent on the front porch while they watched the sun disappear over the hill, then waited for the glorious reds, golds and oranges of a sunset fill the entire sky. Or watching the stars as they filled every bit of inky darkness. Sometimes Clifford, all bundled up, sat between them. Pearl had to laugh. It was as if the baby was their chaperone. Not that they needed one. They were friends, like brother and sister. Didn't everyone know that? Or could some read her mind—know what she was thinking—realize that her heart was shattering. If only she could speak her mind, but she couldn't be bold as Nancy Whitfield was. Never could she speak her heart to Paul. If anyone did any speaking, it would have to be Paul, himself, and of course she knew that would never happen.

After the Drakes were tucked into bed, Pearl sat beside the fire in the dining area and tucked her long legs under her. She had brought some of Emily's books, so now was the time when she would read another chapter from Elsie Dinsmore. She'd read *Black Beauty* twice now and the poem Paul had given her at Christmas many times over.

A new, large library was to be built downtown, across the river. Emily said there would be many books to choose from, and they didn't have to buy; they would be for all to read and enjoy.

The house was quiet and Pearl missed the sounds of family bustling around, the cries and peals of laughter from baby Clifford. She missed seeing Emily write in her journal, seeing Mama sit beside the fire, her hands busy with knitting needles. It was probably a sweater she knitted for the baby. Or perhaps new mittens for Emily—or maybe Ben or Paul.

Finally Pearl took the light and climbed the attic stairs to the bedroom where Emily had once slept. It was sparsely furnished, but the bed was comfortable and the small braided rug was the very one Emily had kneeled on to say her prayers. Pearl bent down now and asked for God to heal Mr. Drake. Asked that Mrs. Drake might ask for Emily, that she'd want to meet her great-grandchild. Pearl was glad about the photo album, but more than anything, she wanted Beulah Drake to give it to Emily.

"Help me to understand, O, Lord, Thy will for my life, also. If it is to be that I will teach here in Portland, or if it is Thy will that I will take care of those who cannot help themselves, I will accept this. I will try to make others happy, for I know, in so doing, I in turn will be happy. Just serving Thee makes me happy. Thy will be done. Amen."

Pearl took out a small volume she kept under her pillow. It was a diary. Emily had suggested she write down her thoughts and so she had tried to do so. She couldn't write for long periods of time as Emily did, but some thoughts came into her mind. Tonight seemed to be one of those times.

My life is full. I am reasonably happy. Just thinking of Paul makes me happy. Seeing his smile erupt across his broad face gives me much pleasure.

I know if there is ever to be anyone for me to love, to marry, to have children with, it is Paul. But perhaps that is not to be my lot in life.

> *As I take up my pen to write*
> *On this, yet another dark, cold night*
> *I think of things that have been and will be*
> *I think of laughter, smiles, tears and joy*
>   *for me*
> *I think of Mary Alice this day*
> *And hope she is loved and cherished.*

Pearl closed the small book and lay back on the pillow. She wondered about the Rome children, especially Mary Alice. What she wouldn't do to bring Mary Alice here to live. Who was to help her to know what it was like being a woman? Who would be there to comb and braid her hair, to listen to her numbers and as she read pages from her reading book? She knew Judson Rome had no interest in what his children did. Perhaps the new teacher would become their mother. Perhaps she, Pearl, was silly to even think of such things, much less worry about them. There wasn't anything she could do. Then a thought hit. She could write to them. She would borrow paper from Mrs. Drake and have a letter ready to go on Monday morning. Yes, she must know how everything was in Stayton. She must let them know how much she missed them. And she might even write to the new teacher, whomever she was and tell her that her prayers were with her, that she would find happiness there and please the school board.

Pearl closed her diary and blew out the flame. Tomorrow would be another busy day with carrying water, building a fire and making tea. Lots of tea.

thirteen

One morning two weeks later, after Mrs. Drake refused the oatmeal Pearl brought, Pearl took it away without a word.

"I prefer the green glass bowls," Beulah said, then started coughing.

Pearl took the tray back to the kitchen and transferred the cereal to a green bowl. Soon she returned to the bedroom with a daffodil in a small vase. Perhaps a touch of spring would raise the woman's spirits.

Beulah took one look at the flower and frowned. "I don't need a daffodil on my tray."

"Very well." Pearl removed the daffodil and stuck the vase on the dresser.

"Does anything bother you?" Beulah asked.

Pearl turned and looked at the older woman. "Yes, many things, but I pray about them and soon the bother passes."

"Thee is a special person," Beulah said then. "Most people can't stand me."

Pearl smiled. "I just think of thee as one of my pupils at school where I taught. He didn't like me. He said nasty things about me, but I won him over. I read to him."

Beulah's face lit up. "I don't know if I like being compared to a naughty child, but I like the reading part."

"Oh. Would thee like me to read?"

"Yes, please."

Pearl sat, facing Beulah Drake. The once bright eyes were dull; lifeless. The doctor had come, at Ben's insistence, and said she wouldn't last another month. Pearl had walked him to the door.

"It's tuberculosis. Though some say a cure is possible, I've not seen it happen in any of the cases I'm familiar with."

Pearl thought of Mama. Had he given the same prognosis for her?

Somehow she didn't want to ask, didn't want to know. Mama had to live a good many more years.

"Is it contagious?" Pearl asked then.

"We cannot be sure. Again, some studies indicate one might catch it, but it depends on the immune system and whether it can be fought."

Pearl was suddenly thankful for her strong constitution, her height and large-boned frame.

Pearl took the well-worn Bible in her hand. "Does thee have a favorite passage?"

The head nodded. "Please read from 1 Corinthians," her voice went low. "I believe it's chapter 13."

Pearl's voice filled the otherwise still room, pausing in the right places.

"'If I have not love, I am but a clanging cymbal. . .'" She paused, then read on. "'. . .the greatest of these is love.'"

Beulah reached out. "Read that passage once again, child."

Pearl read the chapter twice and when she had finished

she noticed a tear had slipped down the lined, pale cheek.

"I find that chapter especially gratifying," Pearl said, not knowing what else to do. Should she offer her a handkerchief, or pretend she didn't see the tears? Beulah was proud; far be it from Pearl to offend in any way.

Beulah sniffed and Pearl moved closer. "Perhaps a cup of tea would be refreshing."

"Thee knows my granddaughter, Emily."

"Yes, I know. . .her."

"Emily planted those daffodil bulbs. She liked flowers and Christmas trees, singing and playing the organ. This house has not heard music since she left."

"Emily has a piano now."

Beulah's eyebrows raised. "I'm sure she must be pleased about that."

"Yes, she is."

"People do not understand how it was with Emily."

"Perhaps not." Pearl always answered, because if she didn't, Beulah would demand a comment.

"She came to us at age ten. . . ." She began coughing and, once started, had a problem stopping.

Pearl leaned forward. "Take thy time, Mrs. Drake."

"She was the oldest of eight at the time."

"A large family."

"They—that is my son worked the fields. Traveled from place to place, picking crops." Beulah coughed again and Pearl leaned over and fluffed the pillows, holding her head as she rose to try to get rid of the phlegm in her throat.

Finally she had stopped. Her fingers clutched the top

of the quilt. "My son could have worked elsewhere, but I'm sorry to say, he let his family work. And they worked many hours, especially during the summer months."

Pearl swallowed hard. She had never heard this much from Emily. In fact, she wasn't sure Emily even knew about it. If so, she'd never said.

"I—offered to take Emily because she was a mite sickly."

"She was?"

"Oh, yes. She fainted out in the fields, and once they had to take her to the hospital, so my son asked if she could come here. Live with us."

"And that was many years ago?"

Beulah raised a hand to her forehead, looking as if she was in pain. "I think it must have been nigh on to eighteen years ago now. If thee must know the truth, I cannot remember exactly."

"Emily spoke of missing her mother."

"Yes, she often asked to go on the train to visit—"

"And she did go—before she married Ben."

"That is good to know."

"Do you want to make amends?" Pearl asked. She knew if it was going to happen, the time was short and it should be done as soon as possible. She also knew that Emily longed more than anything to see her grandparents again, to know that all was forgiven. Perhaps not forgotten, but truly forgiven.

Beulah nodded; her hands gripped the binding on the sheet. She looked away then, as if fighting back tears. "I never told her how much I cared for her. And I want to see her baby. I hear she has one."

"I can fetch her here."

Pearl wished the grandfather was better, but since the stroke, he knew nobody, and lay lifeless and listless in his bed, not even acknowledging Pearl when she fed him. Pearl knew, too, that it was Emily he loved so much.

Pearl rose. "I will see what I can do. Another person is coming tomorrow to take care of things. I will speak to your Emily."

Beulah clutched her hand. "You are a nice person."

Pearl couldn't believe it as she took the dinner dishes to the kitchen. Beulah wanting to see Emily and the baby. Of course she hadn't mentioned Ben, but Ben would understand. He was good about things like that. He would want this for Emily, knowing how happy it would make her. And baby Clifford. His fat little cheeks and rosebud mouth would please any great-grandparent. He laughed a lot, was a noisy child and if anyone could bring a smile to Beulah's face, it would be him. And perhaps the grandfather would even take note. It was something to hope for.

As she washed and rinsed the dishes, Pearl wondered how Paul was, what he was doing this very moment. Tomorrow she'd see him in church. She could hardly wait. It was difficult when she only saw him once a week, but perhaps it was better that way. Her heart remembered, and her mind was full of memories—his smile, the laugh, the way he called her "Gem" and the way he smelled and looked after working all day. Dirty, unkempt, but she loved it anyway. Would the day ever come when he might know how she felt? Was there a chance? Pearl dried her hands and went down the hall to the grandfather's bedroom. He lay still, staring up at the ceiling.

"Hello, Mr. Drake. Did you know your granddaughter Emily is coming to visit tomorrow?" Pearl smiled. "Well, I can't say absolutely, but I think it will happen. I know she wants to see you—"

She stopped. Did his left hand flutter just a bit? Wouldn't that be something if Emily could bring a few happy moments back into the old man's life? Pearl tucked the covers in and adjusted his pillow. "Thee rest well tonight. If thou needs me during the night, call out if thou can."

Pearl checked once more on Beulah. The heavy quilt rose up and down in rhythmic tones, the labored breathing filling the room. Pearl leaned over and said a quick prayer. "And if it pleases Thee, Lord, help this to work out well in the morning."

Pearl tiptoed up the steep stairway, lamp in hand. Though most people now had electricity in their homes, the Drakes clung to the old ways. They still pumped their water from a well and used kerosene lamps. It was dark and cold in the small bedroom. She went to her knees and prayed for God's will to be done. So much had happened. Emily had left, without notice, because she knew she could not stay if she were to marry Ben, a non-Quaker, but a God-fearing man, nevertheless. And her grandmother had forbidden her to ever come back again, disowning her. But Emily felt God led her to Ben. And she left, not looking back once.

"O God, you know how Emily tried to make peace.

She invited her grandparents to the wedding, but they refused. Just as they refused to come when she was expecting a baby. And that baby died, and now there is Clifford. O please let it all end happily. Amen."

fourteen

Pearl waited for the horses to come fetch her for Seventh Day Meeting. A nurse, someone Ben had hired, had come to stay with the Drakes on Sunday. Pearl showed her where everything was and gave her instructions about which cup Beulah preferred to drink out of and passed on other little hints.

Pearl slipped on her best gray muslin, tied her braids into a thick knot and glanced at her face in the mirror in Emily's old room.

"O God, I may not be the most beautiful woman, but Emily and Mama say that looks don't count; it's what's in the heart that does and I thank You for my blessings."

She heard the sound of horses hooves coming up the lane and hurried down the steps and opened the door just as a knock sounded.

Paul stood, grinning as he held out his arm to Pearl. "I understand you are in need of a ride this morning and Ben suggested I could pick you up for church. That is, if you don't mind."

"Oh!" Pearl was so surprised words couldn't escape past the lump in her throat. "I—expected Ben—I thought you were off working on a new house—"

"Well, I can see you are not pleased to see me, but I think thee will be happy to ride behind my new team of horses."

"Oh, Paul, you didn't!" Pearl clasped her hands as she ran out to look at the new team. "They're absolutely beautiful!"

"Pandy and Mandy," he said. "Bought 'em yesterday."

"Oh," Pearl said again. "I would adore riding to church behind such a gorgeous team!"

Paul helped her up into the carriage and Pearl smoothed her skirt down and adjusted her bonnet. Her heart thudded against her rib cage and she wondered if it would ever slow down. He lifted the reins and they were off.

Pearl felt a bit awkward sitting next to Paul, then remembered the news and knew she must tell him. Especially since they were his grandparents, too.

"Grandma Drake wants to see Emily and baby Clifford."

"Pearl, are you sure?" Paul let the reins slip for a minute. "Is this true?"

"We talked for at least an hour and she—I could hardly believe it—she was crying."

"Oh, Gem, this is wonderful. This is what Emily has been praying about."

"I know." Pearl smiled. She liked it when Paul called her by the nickname. It had come out so easily, almost as if he had been rehearsing it. She felt comfortable. At last. It was like the old times. Times when they had talked on the porch, counted the stars, eaten apple pie together. They had been friends then and maybe that's all they would ever be, but it would be enough. Pearl could manage it somehow.

"What're you grinnin' about?" Paul asked suddenly,

poking her in the ribs.

"Just thinking about how things are working out and it's just like in the Bible. 'All things work together for good to them that love God.'"

Paul's face clouded over for a brief moment. "I guess that's right, Gem, but I don't know if it applies to everyone."

"Of course it does, Paul Michael Drake."

He laughed. "You get the cutest look on your face when you get riled up."

Pearl felt her face flush. "I'm not riled up."

"Are, too."

"I should know if I am or not." She tightened the strings of her bonnet and knew she was acting like a little girl, not the adult woman she wanted to be. The woman God intended for her to be.

"I should think you'd believe in God considering all the things he's done for you."

"Such as?"

"Bringing you here to Oregon, giving you a fine job, a house to live in, food to eat. What more could any one person want?"

"A woman to have his children?"

Pearl's face colored more than before. "I—well—that is—maybe you have a point." She looked away, not wanting Paul to see the color of her cheeks, the way her eyes had misted over. He must never know how she really felt—he would really laugh then.

"Are you going to go back to teaching?" he asked then.

"I have considered it."

"And?"

"I'm not sure if that's what I should do."

"Go where your heart leads you. Isn't that what Luke would say?"

He ran a hand through his thick, sandy hair. Pearl wanted to reach up and touch the one lock that kept falling onto his forehead.

She nodded. "I guess that's what I'm having a problem about."

She avoided Paul's gaze. "The man I marry someday must love God with all his heart and soul."

Paul was silent for a long moment. "I hope you find what you're looking for, Pearl."

The light banter of minutes before was now punctuated by silence, and Pearl wanted to take her words back. Why couldn't Paul understand God was the master of the universe, that He was in control of every facet of a person's life? Why did he struggle so? Why didn't he just try harder to understand the principles of faith, to trust that things would work out?

"Looks like we're here," Paul said, commanding his horses to a halt. Pearl didn't wait to be helped, but gathered her skirts and jumped down. "Thank you very much for the ride." She hesitated. "I'm glad you came to pick me up this morning." Before Paul could answer, she hurried inside, eager to tell Emily the wonderful news.

Ben, Emily, and baby Clifford were already in church. Pearl nearly raced down the aisle to the pew.

"Where's Mama?" she asked, nearly forgetting her message when she failed to see her mother sitting next to Ben.

"Mama's not good this morning," Ben said.

Pearl felt the tightness return as it did lately when she thought about her mother. "I should go see her this afternoon." Then she remembered her mission.

"Emily, you must come to the Drake's this afternoon after church."

Emily stared at her sister-in-law. "What are you saying?"

"Mrs. Drake has asked for you. She told me lots of things and how she cared about you—always had—and—"

"When should Emily go?" Ben interrupted.

"She said it was time to forgive, that her time is running out."

"Oh, Ben," Emily turned to look at her husband and her mouth quivered. "Have my prayers been answered?"

"Rather looks that way."

Pearl sat, offering to hold the baby. She'd missed him so terribly during the months she lived in Stayton and even more so now that she'd been staying with the Drakes. She held his face next to her own, repeating the prayer she'd offered to God many times before. "O God, if is Thy will, please let me have a child someday. And if it isn't asking too much, let it be Paul's child."

The service started, but Pearl was much too excited to concentrate. Besides, Paul sat in back of her and she could feel him watching her every move. She decided from now on she'd sit behind him.

fifteen

Pearl held baby Clifford as she and Emily stood on the front porch of the Drake home. Paul had brought them over from meeting and was tying the team to a post while Ben went home to see how Sarah was.

Emily grasped her hand for a long moment. "I don't know what to do, Pearl. It's been so long since I walked in this door."

"She's expecting you. Just go in and give her one of your best smiles and say—well—say hello. The rest is up to your grandmother."

Emily nodded. "You're right. I'll act as if I'd never been gone."

The door opened and the nurse peered out. "You must be Emily."

Emily stepped forward, her hands gripping the sides of her coat. "Yes, I am. Is my—grandmother ready to receive company?"

The nurse smiled. "Mrs. Drake has been expecting you. As for the mister, he just stares at the wall or ceiling. Won't be no recognition in those eyes."

Emily tried to stifle the pain deep inside her chest. She wanted this to be over. Clifford let out a noise and Pearl held a finger to his mouth. "Sh-h—, baby boy."

"Here, let me take him." Emily reached for her robust six-month-old. "Please don't cry, my son."

The nurse led them down the hall, not that she had to lead the way for either one. Pearl entered the room first and Beulah turned slightly. "Has she come? I thought I heard a baby's cry."

"Thee did, Grandmother." Emily entered the room and turned the baby around to face his great-grandmother. "This is my son, Clifford. I wish you could hold him, but he's a handful."

It was dark inside, as the light bothered Beulah's eyes. "Thee can come closer."

Emily moved to the head of the bed and held out her son. Clifford laughed and pulled at the nightcap Beulah wore.

"My, but thee's a fine, strapping young boy!"

"That he is, Grandmother."

"And thee. Look at thee. A sight for sore eyes. Never thought I'd see thee again, child."

Emily handed Clifford to Pearl, leaned over the bed and kissed her grandmother's cheek. Tears shone in both eyes. "Nor I thee."

"Come. Sit. Tell me about thy life. We've got some catching up to do."

Was that it, Pearl wondered. No words saying she was sorry? Of course Beulah Drake was a proud woman and even in her sickness she would hold her head as high as possible.

"We lost our Isobelle."

"Yes, I heard."

"We decided—Ben and I—to try for another child. And here he is."

The squirming child tried to be free.

"I think he might be hungry," Emily said then. "That might calm him down enough to take a nap."

❧

"Is Benjamin here?"

Emily's eyes widened. "Oh, Grandmother, I did not think thee wanted to see Ben."

"Humph! He's thy husband and thee does love him and are making a home for him?"

"Of course."

"Then I want to see him."

Emily looked shocked, then a slight smile turned up at the corner of her mouth. "Thee will see him. I will send Paul after him."

"I will tell Paul to fetch Ben," Pearl said. "I may ride with him as I'm worried about Mama."

"Yes, go," Beulah said. "I have plenty of care now."

Clifford's chatter and the women's voices filled the house as Pearl slipped out the front door.

❧

"I was wrong not to forgive thee, child," Beulah whispered, then the rasping cough began again. "Thee followed thy heart and God has given thee a good man, a righteous husband."

"Oh, Grandmother." Tears squeezed out of Emily's eyes, falling down on top of Clifford's head. How long she had waited to hear those very words, prayed for forgiveness and that she could see her grandparents once more before they died:

The calloused hand gripped the small, thin one. "Thee always has been a puny little thing."

Emily smiled through her tears. "And thee has been

strong and stout and can I say a bit feisty?"

"Determined." Grandma Beulah nodded. The gray hair fanned across the pillow and Emily reached out and touched it.

"I love thee," she whispered.

"And I love thee."

The two women sat in silence as the sun poked through the windows, lighting the two figures who sat close together, neither speaking because words were no longer necessary.

"Thee needs to play the organ," Beulah said, breaking the silence. "I need to hear thee play once again."

"Soon as I have fed Clifford."

Clifford nursed and minutes later his head bobbed in complete relaxation.

"Here. I shall make a bed for him on the floor, then see Grandfather before playing."

"A spot of tea before thou goes," Beulah said then.

Emily brought the tea, went to her grandfather's room and held his hand for the longest moment. No movement, no recognition, though she spoke his name several times.

She left the room, tears coursing down her cheeks again as she went to the parlor where the old organ sat in a corner.

She would play everything she knew. She would once again fill this house with music and song. And she might even sing along too.

Paul saw Pearl approach and hopped down from the buggy. "Is something wrong?"

"Oh, no." Pearl tried to calm the tremor in her voice.

"Everything—oh, Paul, everything is very fine."

"Oh, thank goodness. I was worried."

Pearl looked at this lean face, the eyes that went from troubled to light. How she loved those eyes, the steady gaze, the man standing before her, but she could not speak her heart, her mind.

"You are to go after Ben. Your grandmother wishes to see him."

"Now?"

Pearl nodded, and pushed a pin back into the braid at the nape of her neck. "Yes. Now. "

"That looks as if it pleases you very much."

"It pleases Emily and what pleases my dear sister-in-law pleases me."

Paul looked with longing for only a moment, then climbed into he buggy. "Do you want to come with me?"

"Yes," she replied without a moment's hesitation. She felt her face burning under his strong gaze.

"Your coming will make the trip more pleasant. Unless you need to stay to take care of Clifford."

"No," Pearl answered a bit too quickly. "Emily will put him down for a nap—after he has his milk."

"Then let's go." Paul hopped down again, gave his arm to Pearl and helped her into the high seat beside him. She was tall; broad-shouldered, but she was also graceful and the smile she wore on her face constantly pleased him.

"Thy grandfather stays the same," Pearl said as they headed west. "I fed him earlier and he's now asleep."

"He's earned his rest." Paul turned and looked at the

firm chin, the way her face shone in the afternoon sun. The bonnet cast shadows across her features.

Paul had come to help bathe his grandfather. He also took turns sitting beside him and had read to him. Nothing had worked. There were no signs that he understood anything going on around him.

"Perhaps if my grandparents have forgiven Emily she will come to stay with them now."

"I think they—that is—Grandmother Drake would like that very much."

The sun beaming into the small carriage made Pearl's heart sing with sudden joy. She had thoughts that burst inside her from time to time and usually there was no one to share them with. Today she had Paul and without a second thought, she began singing in her clear, high voice.

> *What a friend we have in Jesus,*
> *All our hopes and grieves to bear.*
> *What a privilege to carry*
> *Everything to the Lord in prayer.*

"You believe that, don't you?" Paul's hand let up on the rein. For right now he wanted to stop the carriage, wanted to stop time, wanted Pearl's voice to go on singing. It was as if she was meant to be here beside him. He'd never felt more sure of anything in his whole life.

"I believe God answers prayer, yes."

"And you've prayed for a change of heart in Grandmother."

"I have."

"And Emily and Ben have."

"Don't forget Luke and Kate. It's been a long time in coming, Paul."

Paul let the reins fall the rest of the way without fully realizing it. "And if I pray for something I want very much, do you think He will hear me?"

"He always hears us." Pearl turned and looked into his eyes. "It may not be the way you would hope, but He does hear and He does answer prayer."

"But I must first believe."

If Pearl realized they had stopped, she did not let on. "Thee may believe more than thee realize, my brother."

Brother. There was that term Pearl and the other Friends used. By her answering his question with the term, he knew she still felt he was part of the family. Nothing more.

"Does thee want to tell me what the prayer is about? It could be that others have this same prayer on their mind and hearts—"

"No," Paul interrupted. "I'm afraid not."

Pearl leaned over for one of the reins, without looking into Paul's eyes again. "Very well, then. I think we'd better pick up Ben, don't you?"

The rest of the trip was spent in silence. Pearl's smile had changed to a look of seriousness. She wished she knew what Paul was thinking, what he prayed for, but she would not, could not pry. She wondered if it had anything to do with Nancy Whitfield.

Ben sat on the front porch, whittling. The roses bloomed along the fence he'd put up a few weeks ago

in anticipation of baby Clifford's learning to walk and
wanting to go outside to play. He would be safe from
the harm of the street, ever growing with daily traffic—
he and the animals the Galloways owned.

"Yahoo!" he called, standing. "What's going on? I
expected Emily and Clifford to be with you."

Pearl hopped down, not waiting for Paul to assist her,
and ran to her brother. "The most wonderful thing has
happened," she said, her eyes dancing. "An answer to
many, many prayers!"

Ben cupped his chin. "And what might that be?"

Sarah came onto the porch, shielding her face from
the warm sun. "Goodness, gracious, what has happened?" A spasm hit her and she nearly doubled over
from sudden coughing.

"Oh, Mama, Emily is with her grandmother, who
wants Ben to come. Isn't it wonderful?"

After a glass of water, Sarah assured Pearl she would
be fine and insisted Pearl return with Ben and Paul. In
her hands were a loaf of freshly baked bread and a pie
to help with the celebration.

The two men chatted from the front seat, but Pearl
found herself staring at the back of Paul's head. He had
a cowlick and she knew no matter how hard he tried to
train it, the hair refused to lie down. She wanted to
reach out and smooth the stubborn hair down, but
refrained. He might not like it.

Her thoughts scampered through her mind as the old
farmhouse, now even more weathered gray than when
Emily lived there, came into view. Soon there would be
even more reunion and perhaps with all the noise and

celebration, Grandfather Drake might recognize his world and loved ones once again.

The door opened and Emily ran out.

"Oh, Ben. Paul. Pearl. I played the organ, Grandfather's favorite tune: 'Count Thy Blessings,' and tears rolled down his cheeks. I saw it with my very own eyes."

"And Clifford?" Ben jumped down, handing the reins to Paul.

"He's slept through it all. Of course he's used to my playing the piano at home."

"Oh, we have so much to be thankful for," Ben said, walking toward the house.

"Yes, we do," Pearl answered, falling in step beside Ben. "He does answer prayers, doesn't He?" She stole a quick glance at Paul, but he did not return her look.

sixteen

Within minutes, Ben and Paul had carried Grandfather into the parlor, where Pearl propped his head with pillows and covered his limp figure with a heavy quilt from his bed.

"Play, Emily. Play more hymns. He's responding. Thank God, he's responding."

Beulah Drake could barely walk, but she managed to make it to the parlor, where she sat in the Victorian chair. Her body was wracked with coughing, but she smiled, though clutching her chest.

"I never thought I'd see the day when our parlor would be full of people, Emily playing and others singing."

Pearl's voice, Paul's deep bass and Ben's tenor soon filled the small room. A hand reached out as if Harrison Drake were trying to reach his granddaughter. Through tears, Emily played all the hymns she knew by heart, the ones she had played over the years, the ones that meant so much to her and those of her loved ones.

A sudden wail sounded from the bedroom floor where Clifford had been napping.

"I'll get him," Pearl said. "You keep on playing."

"He just wants to sing, too," Ben said.

"That child will never be left out when there's a party or singing going on."

"'Rock of Ages Cleft for me, Let me hide myself in thee.'"

Emily went from hymns to other old favorites: "Jeannie with the Light Brown Hair," "O Susanna," and "I've Been Working on the Railroad."

Grandfather had moved his right arm and appeared to be keeping time to the music.

"Look, Emily," Pearl cried. "He's trying to smile."

"Thee has brought such joy into this house again." Beulah shook her head. "So much hurt."

"This is turning into a regular prayer meeting," Ben said. "I think we should offer a prayer of thanks to our God for His wonderful mercy to us."

Pearl bowed her head and sensed Paul was watching her. She wanted to reach out, take his hand, tell him it was okay. Everything was going to be all right.

Later there was coffee, tea, Emily's cherry pie, and an apple pie that Pearl had made the day before. Pearl sliced the fresh bread Emily had made on Saturday and some of Sarah's raisin cake.

"God forgives and so should I," Grandmother Drake said then.

It was late afternoon when Pearl cleaned up the dishes, Ben and Paul carried Grandfather back to bed and tucked him in and Beulah was back in her bed.

"I will come often, Grandmother," Emily said. "I can come and let Pearl go home."

"If that is thy wish, then it is mine, also."

The two clung for a long moment, then Emily left on Ben's arm.

Clifford had fallen asleep in Paul's arms in the big

chair by the wood stove. "I think this one needs to go home."

Pearl watched the little family make their way to the buggy and closed the door. It had been the most glorious day she could remember and her heart leapt inside her. How good forgiveness feels. How beautiful Beulah looked. How peaceful Harrison was. This day would not soon be forgotten.

ᘒ

The following week was busy. Emily came by on Monday, Wednesday and Friday. She played each day and Pearl left to go home to be with Mama. Clifford stayed with Emily, sleeping in his own little bed. Memories were made. Kind words were spoken and Grandfather had even said a word: Emily. It was difficult to understand, but Emily knew it was her name and gave him a squeeze.

On the tenth day following the reunion, Harrison Drake slipped away in his sleep. He'd gone to be with his Lord one week when Beulah closed her eyes one night and did not wake up.

Luke came for both services. They were services of celebration.

Kate came and embraced Emily. "God calls those home he needs. And Beulah had made her peace."

Sarah had more times of coughing than not and Pearl and Ben knew she'd be called home soon, too. But Pearl couldn't bear to think about it.

A letter arrived on April fourteenth. Anna was coming west, and she was coming to stay. At least Sarah would see one more child before she died.

seventeen

It was May, a few weeks after the first funeral, and Pearl had come home. Home to be with Sarah. In a weakened condition, she lay on her bed, accepting the meals brought to her, yet not wanting anyone to fuss over her.

"I'm going to be all right. You go fuss with the baby."

Pearl sat beside her mother and stroked her hair. "Mama, I cannot bear to see you like this."

"I know, child." Her hand reached for her youngest child. "I would never cause thee any pain, if I could help it. I have but one request before I go to be with my Lord."

"What is it, Mama? I'll do anything I can."

"I want to know that thou are settled in life. Here you are doing for every one, tending to the sick, teaching children, but what is it that you want?"

Pearl knew, had always known she wanted to marry, have children, to serve God—to be as happy as Emily and Ben, Kate and Luke. Yet God's plan still wasn't clear in her mind.

"Has thee asked for the desires of thy heart?"

Pearl looked away.

"As I thought."

"Mama, the person I have strong feelings for does

not believe. He has said as much."

"Often people say they do not believe, when they do. It takes longer for some to recognize God's goodness, His faithfulness. I feel it to be so in this situation."

Pearl felt uncomfortable. She didn't like it when the attention was on her. She wanted to help others; she was a server as Luke had said the day he drove her to the Drake's farmhouse.

"Mama, do you want a cup of tea?"

"Do not evade the issue," Sarah said.

"I'm not."

"You answered too quickly."

"I just want to make you feel better."

"Then sing for me. Thy voice is so clear. So beautiful. I can well imagine it is as the angels singing in heaven."

Pearl grasped her mother's hand, and tried to hold back the tears. "'Be Thou my vision, O Lord of my heart.'"

Pearl sang all the hymns she knew from memory, and when the words wouldn't come, she hummed. The creases on Sarah's forehead faded as a smile came to her lips. It was as if she were ready now. Ready to go home and Pearl was leading the way.

The doctor came that day. He shook his head. "There is nothing more to do for her. Keep her warm. Comfortable. Give her clear broth. Her body cannot digest more."

Pearl read, sang then talked about the farm in Iowa and what she remembered about her father.

"Mama, I remember that little chest Papa made. How

thee loved it. And you were so happy you could bring it on the train to Oregon."

Sarah smiled, as if recalling earlier days, making a home for Jeb, the arrival of her babies. Each child was an added blessing. And God had blessed her even more by giving her grandchildren. She touched Pearl's arm. "Read the passage from Matthew."

Pearl knew the one Sarah meant. It was well marked in her Bible:

> *"Come unto me, all ye that labour and are*
> *   heavy laden,*
> *and I will give you rest.*
> *Take my yoke upon you, and learn of me;*
> *for I am meek and lowly in heart:*
> *and ye shall find rest unto your souls.*
> *For my yoke is easy, and my burden is*
> *   light."*

Sarah squeezed Pearl's hand. "That is the one. I will give you rest. I am not ready for the passage in John quite yet. I am waiting for my Anna to come." She closed her eyes and Pearl slipped from the room. Though she tried to tell herself that Mama would live forever, she knew it could not happen. This consumption had taken over her body, and it would be a matter of days, possibly hours.

Pearl washed her hands thoroughly before starting the bread for tomorrow. Everyone could be susceptible to contracting tuberculosis, but if caution was taken, the household would survive. "God giveth and God taketh away" went through her mind. And Mama was ready to go. Her words of today indicated she knew her fate and she was preparing herself.

The kitchen was quiet with Emily and Clifford napping. Pearl opened the window and felt the spring breeze on her face. This home, this place meant so much to her. Yet Mama was right. What was she to do about the desires of her heart?

Kneading the bread was balm for her soul. She punched and turned and punched it down more.

"My, but that will be the lightest bread we've had in quite a while." Emily stood in the doorway, smiling.

"Yes—I guess I got carried away."

"How is Mama?"

"Resting for now."

"I'll take the next shift, Pearl. You need to get away."

Get away. Was that what was needed? If she were to go, where would it be?

When dinnertime came and Paul hadn't arrived home, Ben said they should eat anyway. "He's probably finishing up the Powell house."

Pearl was cutting pie, and Sarah had finished a whole cup of clear broth and was resting again, when the phone call came.

"It's Judson Rome," Emily said, looking at Pearl.

Pearl's face turned white, the knife slipping from her hand. *Judson Rome? What could he want?* "I don't want to talk to him."

"Hear what the man has to say," Ben said.

Pearl reached for the receiver, a hundred thoughts whirling through her mind. Was it about teaching?

What else? He already knew she would say no to another marriage proposal. She cleared her throat. "This is Pearl Galloway."

The voice sounded strange, almost hollow. "Miss Galloway, Judson Rome here."

"Yes?"

"I am in an awkward position and thought of you immediately. I know I can count on you."

"What is it, Mr. Rome?" No matter how many times he had told her to call him "Judson," she had never been comfortable doing so and wasn't about to do so now.

"I need a teacher for the fall term. I realize that's several months away, but the school board does like to prepare in advance."

"I am hardly a viable candidate," she said, feeling the shock from his request. "Have you forgotten your words?"

There was a long pause, but she knew he was there. She could hear his breathing. Her hand reached for the chair as she eased into it. All eyes were on her, watching, waiting.

"Oh, my, no. I was hard on you. I have done some rethinking and after speaking with my sons and Mary Alice, I realize how much they actually learned in the few months you taught at our little school."

It was good to hear that he finally recognized her worth. Still. . . .

"Mary Alice asks for you all the time."

"Is Mary Alice all right?"

"Of course. I remarried and she has a mother at long last."

"Married? Oh, how wonderful, Mr. Rome."

"Yes, well I married the new teacher and we're quite happy."

So that's why he was calling. His wife could no longer teach and with Judson Rome no longer heckling her, Pearl thought it might work. She glanced around the room, at the people she loved the most. Was this the window God was opening? Is this what he wanted her to do?

"What is it?" Ben finally asked, lurching to his feet. "Pearl?"

He took the phone.

"Hello. This is Ben Galloway, Pearl's brother."

Pearl remained motionless. Why couldn't she think straight? Judson Rome needed an answer. He was calling long distance. What was wrong with her?

Emily put a cup of coffee in her hand and the voice stopped. Ben put his arm around her shoulder. "We will return Mr. Rome's call later. After you've had time to consider the teaching position."

"And what you need now is a day off. I think you should get away from this house and have a fun day riding the streetcar, or shopping at the new farmer's market," Emily said.

Wasn't that what Emily had said earlier?

Pearl watched while Clifford banged on his highchair tray. Ben ate his pie and Emily sipped her coffee. Was it time to leave this safe cocoon? Should she go back to teaching?

The back door opened and Paul entered the kitchen. His bulk filled the doorway and her heart nearly stopped. Paul. He was the reason she hesitated, even if only for a moment. She loved him, but it wasn't to be.

"Sorry I'm late." He hesitated, looking around. "Why is it so quiet? You all look—" His eyes widened. "Not Sarah?"

"No," Ben finally answered. "Pearl just got a phone call from Judson Rome. He wants her to return to teaching in the fall."

"Oh." Paul took the plate Emily offered and dished up his dinner. He glanced at Pearl, but she stared, transfixed into space, as if nobody were here.

"Did you finish the job?" Ben asked.

"Yes. It's done. They can move in on Saturday."

"Good. Take the day off tomorrow. I want you to take Pearl on a picnic down by Johnson Creek. It's not a request, but an order."

"It isn't as if I had to decide tonight," Pearl said then. She hadn't heard anything going on around her and spoke to no one in particular.

Emily nodded. "You're right, Pearl. You don't have to decide immediately. I'd think about it for a few days."

Pearl stared at the cup of lukewarm coffee. "I just wish I knew what to do."

"While you're thinking about it, why not go with Paul on a picnic tomorrow?" Ben said.

"Tomorrow?" Pearl looked dazed. "Tomorrow is Friday. It's a work day. I couldn't—I mean he couldn't possibly go—"

"It's all settled," Ben said. "Paul needs some time off, too. He's been working six ten-hour days, and needs to relax, too."

"I'll go on a picnic only if Pearl brings along an apple pie," Paul buttered another slice of bread. "That's what it has to be."

They laughed and soon Pearl was laughing. It felt good to laugh. She forgot the last time she had. Probably not since Christmas when every one had been here and they had all sung Christmas carols around the piano.

"Pie!" Clifford shouted, banging his fork on the tray.

They turned and laughed all the harder.

"Wouldn't you know pie would be his second word?" Emily said, poking an apple into his mouth. "Yes, our son does like sweets."

She lifted him and held him close. "Such a baby you are," she whispered against his soft, blond hair.

&

Pearl's Princely Apple Pie

6 medium tart apples
3/4 cup sugar
1 tsp. cinnamon
2 tablespoons flour
2 tablespoons heavy cream (set aside)

Peel, quarter and slice apples into a bowl. Cover with sugar, sprinkle on cinnamon and dredge in the flour. Set aside while making the pie crust.

Pearl always used lard for a flakier crust.

2 cups white flour
1 tsp salt
3/4 cup lard
5 tablespoons cold water

Place flour and salt into large bowl. Add lard and cut into flour until mixture resembles small peas. Add the cold water. Divide in half. Roll out bottom crust on a lightly floured board, using a floured rolling pin. Handle as little as possible. Don't try to make it perfectly round. Put in 9" pie pan. Dump in apples. Roll out top crust, making sure it's an inch larger in diameter than pie plate. Before putting on top of apples, pour the heavy cream over apples evenly. Put on top crust. Tuck under bottom crust and crimp edges.

Bake in 400⁰ oven about 45 minutes. Put cookie sheet under pie plate to catch drippings as apples expand as they cook and pie can run over.

Cut into six generous wedges. Top with ice cream, or pass a pitcher of heavy cream. Some prefer a slice of cheddar cheese. Enjoy!

eighteen

The Friday morning began with a clear blue sky without a trace of clouds.

"A perfect day for a picnic," Emily said, packing leftover fried chicken, a jar of dill pickles, bread and butter, and of course two wedges of apple pie left over from last night.

"I shouldn't leave Mama," Pearl protested, but Emily wouldn't hear of it.

"I am so much better now that the morning sickness has gone. I can handle Clifford and Mama just fine." She pointed toward the door. "I'll not hear another word from you except good-bye."

Pearl placed a blanket on top of the picnic basket and checked to see if Paul was finished patching the shed roof.

Paul came around the side of the shed, whistling. It was good to have a day off and he couldn't think of a better way to spend it than with Pearl. He knew she worried about Sarah, hoped that sister Anna would arrive soon and that Emily would have a healthy baby. And now the call from Judson Rome. She liked teaching. She loved the children. He sensed this was her calling; what God intended for her to do.

He'd thought a lot about God the past few weeks. He could see how one was guided by his belief that God would show him the way, and care for him once that path was taken. A lot of the Scriptures made sense, though he often had to read a passage two and three times before he understood it. He had also started praying—a sort of out loud talking prayer when he was alone at night. He thought about moving on. If Pearl left, there was no reason to stay. He wanted to marry, and Pearl always came to mind when he thought of marriage, but if teaching was where God wanted her, far be it for him to stand in the way. Yes, he worried about things, also, but worry seemed to weigh heavier on women. He had never known why.

Paul changed to his Sunday pants, wore the blue shirt that Pearl had once said she liked and slicked back his hair. After feeding Pandy and Mandy, he was ready. Now if Pearl didn't back out.

She came to the door, picnic basket in hand and smiled. She was lovely in the yellow dress. Yellow like the sunshine; it was his favorite color.

"Are you ready?"

Pearl smiled. "Yes."

"Shall it be down by Johnson Creek?" he asked, assisting her up into the buggy.

"Yes, it's my favorite place."

"I feel I should be working." Paul took the reins.

"I feel the same way."

"You do need to think some things out," Paul said.

"Yes."

Pearl held her hands in her lap, wishing she could relax. Paul was her friend. A brother to her. Why was she finding it difficult to talk? Her feelings were strong and she wished she could take them back and just be his friend again. It was easier that way.

"Pearl, what is it you want to do?"

His question caught her off guard. "I don't know." How could she say how she felt? That she wanted to have a home, children?

"I think you do know. You're afraid of something. Why don't you talk about it?"

"How is Nancy Whitfield?" Pearl hadn't gone to church the past two Sundays. She'd stayed home taking care of Mama.

"Nancy is moving to Seattle."

"Are you taking a job there?"

He stopped, letting the reins fall. Suddenly it all came together. Nancy. She thought he cared for Nancy Whitfield. Didn't she know, couldn't she tell that he thought of her day in and day out? Hadn't the picture at Christmas told her where his feelings lay—that it was her face that filled his thoughts?

"I'm staying right here, Gem."

"You haven't called me 'Gem' in a long while."

"Could be because I haven't seen much of you lately."

"Nor I you."

"Will you be happy in Stayton teaching?" He had to know. If so, he would live with it.

"I suppose so."

They crossed the road, and the horses slowed to a trot as they headed toward the creek.

They found a spot under a maple tree close enough to hear the creek rushing over smooth stones. Nothing more was said while Pearl spread the blanket and set the basket between them. Paul sat and moved the basket to the other side.

"Pearl, God's been showing me a lot of things lately —things I wanted to talk to you about."

She heard the words and wondered if her hearing was going bad. *Was this Paul talking? God had been showing him things?*

"I don't have the strong faith that Ben, Emily or Luke have. I am seeking. Does that make sense?"

Pearl turned and their gaze met in a lingering look. The words wouldn't escape past the knot in her throat so she nodded.

"I know what I want. I've known for a very long time."

"To build houses like Ben?"

Paul felt blinded by the sun overhead. Blinded by the bright yellow of Pearl's dress. Blinded by his love for her. "Yes, I am already doing that."

"What else then?" Her heart was hammering against her rib cage and she tried to still it by clasping her hands tight in front of her.

"When you were away teaching, I was happy for you because I knew you were doing what you wanted to do. I liked writing to you. I enjoyed your letters."

"If you only knew how your letters got me through those days—"

"Pearl," he took her hand and held it tight. "Let me finish or I'll never get it out."

"I tried to like Nancy, but it wasn't right. That's when I first knew God was hearing my thoughts. It was as if He led me away from her. And then it was Christmas and you came home and everyone was happy and laughing and singing and your presence made everything right again. I hadn't known until then—until I heard you laugh, watched you holding baby Clifford, heard your voice singing out, that I never wanted to lose sight of you again. Yet now I fear you are going off to teach again. And it should be that way if it's what you want. Just make sure that you really, truly want it."

Could she have heard right? Was this Paul sitting next to her, saying words she had always hoped to hear, but never thought she would?

His voice was speaking, but she could hardly hear it above the pounding of her heart.

"I have yet to hear what you want. It's your turn, Gem."

She'd lain awake half the night, listening to Clifford's even breathing, thinking she would never have a child of her own, but would mother other children, those she taught in the classroom.

She had accepted this to be God's will for her. She would call Judson Rome to give him her decision. That was the last thought she'd had before she could sleep.

"I know you're a good teacher," he said, as if thinking he had to break the silence.

"Yes, I am a good teacher, Paul."

"And you're a good nurse. Look how you took care of my grandparents when they were so ill. And now Sarah. Perhaps nursing is more of your choosing."

"Perhaps." She needed to say more, but the words were still forming in her mind. Her being was bursting with love for this man beside her. Love that she now knew he felt for her. God had answered her prayers. And in the best way possible. How could she have ever doubted Paul's faith? As Mama had said, "We cannot judge, Pearl Marie."

"My dream," Pearl began, "is not to go into nursing, though I would always be there for my family. It is not to teach, though the children are a special blessing. It is to marry a man whom I love and one who would love me back. One who would agree that God is important and we would serve him and our community. It is the way of the Friends, you know."

"Yes, I know." He had not let go of her hand.

"And I want a whole passel of kids?"

"Passel?"

"It's a southern term." She felt happiness bubble up inside her and it was about to tumble out and encompass them both.

"I have questioned God about my lack of beauty, but I know that beauty does come from within and to deny it is to say to God that he has not made a good creation."

"Oh, Gem. You're beautiful to all of us who love you."

She turned and touched Paul's face. "I have thought of thee for such a very long time. I have loved thee with all my heart, though I tried to deny that love for thee filled my heart and soul."

Paul leaned over, touching Pearl's hair, her cheeks, the strong, determined chin. "I prayed last night that God would direct my path today and show me the way and I think He has. I truly think He has."

Pearl stood, throwing her arms into the air. "Oh! I cannot believe this is happening. I cannot keep from shouting. Laughing!"

Paul jumped up and took her hands. "My Gem, my beauty. Thank you God, for giving you to me. For giving us such love."

The lunch was eaten, and then they watched as children came along and searched for crawdads in the shallow water of the creek.

"I think we need to talk to Luke about marrying us—" Paul began.

"After you ask Ben for my hand." Pearl looked up and laughed. "As if we don't know what he will say."

"Everyone's probably been wondering why this didn't happen sooner."

Pearl nodded. "I think I loved you from that first night you arrived from California."

"I think I loved you since the first time I ate your apple pie."

They stayed until the sun started its descent west, then they picked up the blanket and headed home.

"Love's tender path," Pearl said as the horses trotted down Foster Road.

"What does that mean?" Paul asked.

"It's something Mama said about her and Pa. I just remembered it. It was after he died and she talked about how the path can be narrow and rocky in marriage, but if you truly love one and it's the one God intended for you, the path can be tender."

Paul smiled and took her hand again. He had not yet told her about his design, the house he would build. That would come later. Perhaps tomorrow.

epilogue

The Galloway house once again bustled with activity. With the announcement of Pearl and Paul's plans, Sarah took on a better color. God had answered her fervent prayer: she now knew her youngest would be happy. One look at the couple, and she also knew God would bless this union. Paul was an earnest young man who had accepted the Lord into his life. Pearl, as far as Sarah was concerned, was the cream of the crop.

Kate, though close to the delivery time of her first baby, made the special wedding dress, a white organdy with full skirt and puffy sleeves. Luke would officiate, while Emily played the "Wedding March" and vows were repeated in front of the fireplace just as she and Ben had done three years ago.

Anna arrived two days after Paul announced their plans. A replica of Pearl, only smaller, she bustled through the house as if she'd always lived there. Clifford took to her immediately.

"He's going to be a feisty one," she said, tickling him under the chin. "One of these days I'll find someone and have a baby just like you!"

Anna, in a dress of sea green taffeta would be her sister's maid of honor. "It shouldn't be that an older sister does not marry first."

"Thee will marry," Sarah said. She sat in a chair

close to the window where the June sun filled her weakened body with warmth.

But it was Albert who surprised them all. Arriving in Portland, on the *T. J. Potter*, a passenger boat that carried people from the coast and Astoria down the Columbia River, he showed up on the porch two days before the wedding.

Albert was big and loud with a robust laugh. He hugged Sarah close and said he wouldn't have missed coming for anything. "And now you tell me I'm just in time for the wedding of my baby sister?" He laughed again. "Pretty good timing, if I don't say so myself."

There were more hugs and Emily tossed more potatoes and carrots into the stew.

"Anna," Albert said. "You must come back to the beach with me. I'm on the North Beach Peninsula in Washington State. It's God's country there. We need nurses. Doctors. Teachers." He looked at Pearl. "Fishermen we have!" He laughed again.

Before Pearl could answer, he turned to Paul. "Come up there for your honeymoon. You'll love the place."

Paul grabbed Pearl's hand. "I think a boat ride to the coast is just what we should do!"

"I'm not losing my best plasterer, am I?" asked Ben in all seriousness.

"Oh, no," Paul replied. "We'll be back. This is home."

This is home, Pearl thought. "Yes, this is home. And now I am going to be building my own home. Praises be to God."

That summer, weeks after all the festivities, Sarah went to be with her Lord and Savior. Pearl had read the passage the night before she drifted off to sleep.

"In My Father's house are many mansions.

I go to prepare a place for you.

and if I go and prepare a place for you.

I will come again to receive you to myself."

"I will see you later," Sarah murmured, taking her youngest child's hand. "God be with you."

A Letter To Our Readers

Dear Reader:

In order that we might better contribute to your reading enjoyment, we would appreciate your taking a few minutes to respond to the following questions. When completed, please return to the following:

Rebecca Germany, Managing Editor
Heartsong Presents
P.O. Box 719
Uhrichsville, Ohio 44683

1. Did you enjoy reading *Love's Tender Path*?
   ❑ Very much. I would like to see more books
      by this author!
   ❑ Moderately
      I would have enjoyed it more if _____

      _____

2. Are you a member of **Heartsong Presents**? ❑Yes ❑No
   If no, where did you purchase this book? _____

   _____

3. What influenced your decision to purchase this
   book? (Check those that apply.)

   ❑ Cover   ❑ Back cover copy

   ❑ Title   ❑ Friends

   ❑ Publicity   ❑ Other_____

4. How would you rate, on a scale from 1 (poor) to 5
   (superior), the cover design? _____

5. On a scale from 1 (poor) to 10 (superior), please rate the following elements.

___Heroine   ___Plot

___Hero   ___Inspirational theme

___Setting   ___Secondary characters

6. What settings would you like to see covered in **Heartsong Presents** books?_____

_____

_____

7. What are some inspirational themes you would like to see treated in future books?_____

_____

_____

8. Would you be interested in reading other **Heartsong Presents** titles? ❑ Yes   ❑ No

9. Please check your age range:
   ❑ Under 18   ❑ 18-24   ❑ 25-34
   ❑ 35-45   ❑ 46-55   ❑ Over 55

10. How many hours per week do you read? _____

Name _____

Occupation_____

Address_____

City_____ State_____ Zip_____

Romance is Back
"Inn" Style!

From New England to Hawaii and Canada to the Caribbean, *The Christian Bed & Breakfast Directory* has a romantic home-away-from-home waiting for your pleasure. The 1997-98 edition of the directory includes over 1,400 inns. Choose from secluded cabins, beachfront bungalows, historical mansion suites, and much more.

Relevant information about bed and breakfast establishments and country inns is included, inns that are eager to host Christian travelers like you. You'll find descriptions of the inns and accommodation details, telephone numbers and rates, credit card information, and surrounding attractions that satisfy a variety of interests and ages. Maps are also included to help you plan a wonderful romantic getaway.

608 pages; paperbound; 5" x 8"

·········· Presents ··········

Great Inspirational Romance at a Great Price!

Heartsong Presents books are inspirational romances in contemporary and historical settings, designed to give you an enjoyable, spirit-lifting reading experience. You can choose wonderfully written titles from some of today's best authors like Peggy Darty, Tracie J. Peterson, Colleen L. Reece, Lauraine Snelling, and many others.

When ordering quantities less than twelve, above titles are $2.95 each.

Heart♥ng Presents
Love Stories Are Rated G!

That's for godly, gratifying, and of course, great! If you love a thrilling love story, but don't appreciate the sordidness of some popular paperback romances, **Heartsong Presents** is for you. In fact, **Heartsong Presents** is the *only inspirational romance book club*, the only one featuring love stories where Christian faith is the primary ingredient in a marriage relationship.

Sign up today to receive your first set of four, never before published Christian romances. Send no money now; you will receive a bill with the first shipment. You may cancel at any time without obligation, and if you aren't completely satisfied with any selection, you may return the books for an immediate refund!

Imagine. . .four new romances every four weeks—two historical, two contemporary—with men and women like you who long to meet the one God has chosen as the love of their lives. . .all for the low price of $9.97 postpaid.

To join, simply complete the coupon below and mail to the address provided. **Heartsong Presents** romances are rated G for another reason: They'll arrive *Godspeed!*

YES! Sign me up for Heart♥ng!

NEW MEMBERSHIPS WILL BE SHIPPED IMMEDIATELY!
Send no money now. We'll bill you only $9.97 post-paid with your first shipment of four books. Or for faster action, call toll free 1-800-847-8270.

NAME _____

ADDRESS _____

CITY _____ STATE _____ ZIP _____

MAIL TO: HEARTSONG PRESENTS, P.O. Box 719, Uhrichsville, Ohio 44683
YES 1-97